×××PoRch LiEs×××

PoRch LiEs
TALES OF SLICKSTERS, TRICKSTERS, AND OTHER WILY CHARACTERS

by PATRICIA C. McKISSACK

illustrated by ANDRÉ CARRILHO

schwartz & wade books · new york

Text copyright © 2006 by Patricia C. McKissack
Illustrations copyright © 2006 by André Carrilho

Published in the United States by Schwartz & Wade Books, an imprint of Random House Children's Books, a division of Random House, Inc., New York.

SCHWARTZ & WADE BOOKS and colophon are trademarks of Random House, Inc.

www.randomhouse.com/kids
Educators and librarians, for a variety of teaching tools, visit us at
www.randomhouse.com/teachers

Library of Congress Cataloging-in-Publication Data
McKissack, Pat.
    Porch lies : tales of slicksters, tricksters, and other wily characters /
Patricia C. McKissack ; illustrated by André Carrilho.— 1st ed.
        p.   cm.
    ISBN-13: 978-0-375-83619-0 (trade) — ISBN-13: 978-0-375-93619-7
(lib. bdg.)
    ISBN-10: 0-375-83619-5 (trade) — ISBN-10: 0-375-93619-X (lib. bdg.)
    1. Children's stories, American.   2. African Americans—Juvenile
fiction.   [1. African Americans—Fiction.   2. Short stories.]
I. Carrilho, André, ill.   II. Title.
PZ7.M478693Por 2006
[Fic]—dc22

                                                    2005022048

The text of this book is set in Filosofia and Handwriter.
Book design by Rachael Cole

Manufactured in China

10 9 8 7 6 5 4 3 2 1

First Edition

For my husband, with love
and appreciation
—P. McK.

To my sister, Taíla,
and my brother, Ntanzi
—A.C.

CONTENTS

AUTHOR'S NOTE

Whippoorwills, lightning bugs, and homemade peach ice cream trigger memories of my childhood summers spent at my grandparents' house in Nashville, Tennessee. The squat white-framed house at 3706 Centennial, next to the Tennessee State University power plant, sat comfortably on the property as if it was resting in an easy chair. Looking at the house from a distance, I always imagined that the two side windows, the center door, and the sagging porch formed a big happy face, smiling a welcome to me when I rode my bicycle down the long front walk. Skipping up five steps placed me in my favorite spot—the porch swing. There I could read for hours or listen to someone tell a story about sneaky foxes or things that went bump in the night.

I spent a lot of time listening in those days. In the evenings when dinner was done, the dishes washed, and the dish towels hung out to dry, my grandparents Mama Frances and Daddy James spent the rest of the evening on the porch. Sometimes if there was a baseball game Mama Frances hooked up the radio in the living room window so we could listen to the play-by-play in the cool. We were loyal fans of the Brooklyn Dodgers, the first major-league team to sign a black player—Jackie Robinson. We all cheered loudly each time Jackie came to bat, and we never missed a game.

Sometimes there was a Marian Anderson or a Mahalia Jackson concert on, and while my grandmother listened, my grandfather and I were forbidden to say a word. "Shhhh!" Mama Frances whispered, as if she was actually in Carnegie Hall and didn't want us to disturb anyone. "Listen," she told me, "and remember the sound of greatness."

On those hot summer evenings, it was not uncommon for family members, friends, and neighbors to drop by for a visit. Some were invited and others just stopped when they saw us sitting "out front." My grandmother always had a pitcher of lemonade or iced tea and homemade tea cakes prepared for all visitors.

Some of these visitors loved to tell stories, or porch lies, as we called them—tales of humor and exaggeration told to listeners of all ages gathered together on the porch. When the teller's eyes grew mischievously large and bright and his or her hands became as animated as a puppeteer's, we knew that a porch lie was in the making.

Mama Frances always welcomed us kids to join the circle of grown-ups, with the strict understanding that we were to remain unobtrusive. Somehow we managed to sit still in spite of our excitement.

The radio was shut off and all we could hear was the melodic sound of a storyteller's voice. I was especially delighted when the story was a slickster-trickster tale about some wily character who used his wits to outsmart his opponents. I like to think of each of these slicksters as a cross between a Mississippi bluesman and Brer Rabbit, though there were a few women as well. And whether it was someone fast- or slow-talking, a well-dressed city slicker or an innocent-looking country bumpkin, all were gifted with a silver tongue tarnished by an oily reputation. No matter how bad these characters seemed, however, they managed to charm their victims and disarm their critics with just enough humor to take the edge off their unscrupulousness.

Among the many porch lies I heard, the most memorable were about Pete Bruce, a man my grandfather knew in the 1920s. Pete was sly and devilish, but always funny. Whenever we were unsure of ourselves, or when our ever-changing world collided with our concepts of justice and honesty, Daddy James would summon up Pete Bruce. He used Pete Bruce as a vehicle to teach a value, to encourage us to think critically, or just to entertain us by putting a little joy in an otherwise gray day.

And that is my intent, too.

Although these stories contain the essence of truth, they are fiction from beginning to end. I have drawn from my grandfather's models of the slickster-trickster character, and I have expanded the myths, legends, and historical figures who often appear in the African American oral tradition and placed them in my own original porch lies. Smart and charming Mingo Cass, easygoing Link Murphy, and yes, even prim and proper Mis Martha June are my creations.

So now, let your own imagination take you to the front porch of your mind, much like the porch at my grandparents' house. Find a comfortable spot; pour yourself a glass of lemonade—made with fresh lemons—and enjoy one of my porch lies, just as I savored the ones I heard years ago.

Patricia C. McKissack
Chesterfield, Missouri
2005

WHEN PETE BRUCE CAME TO TOWN

Dedicated to Daddy James,
who introduced us to Pete
Bruce at the old house on
Centennial Boulevard in
Nashville, Tennessee

Mis Martha June was a person I thought
*incapable of telling a porch lie. I was wrong. Always prim and proper,
she was a churchgoing woman who spoke in quiet, refined tones with her
mouth pursed in the shape of a little O. She was never without a dainty
pocket handkerchief tucked in her sleeve, which she gingerly used to dab
perspiration from her brow. A woman of Mis Martha June's qualities did
not sweat.*

*She owned a bakery that was known for having the best coconut
cream pies in the world—same recipe her mother used, and her mother
before her. And no customer was more faithful than a wily character
named Pete Bruce, about whom she loved to tell stories. He was considered the prince of confidencers, and the idea of Mis Martha June having
anything to do with the likes of him was about as odd as a fox and a hen
striking up a friendship.*

Porch Lies

"Pete Bruce was the worst somebody who ever stood in shoes," Mis Martha June always began in her quiet manner. But then she'd add quickly, "I'll be the first to admit, however, he could make me laugh in spite of myself, especially when he threw one of his million-dollar smiles my way. . . ."

Here is the rest of the story as she told it long ago on our front porch, on a late-summer night.

I was near 'bout ten years old when I first laid eyes on Pete Bruce. He was a full-fledged rascal and I knew it! If you went by looks alone, Pete Bruce was pleasing enough. Had a nice grade of hair, wore it slicked back with Murray's hair dressing oil and water; had plum black skin, even darker eyes, and a devil-may-care swagger. As I recollect, he always loved big Stetson hats, flashy cars, and loud suits. Stood out. Pete Bruce liked that—standing out, being noticed and all.

Mama sold coconut cream pies to passengers at the bus station back then, and her reputation as a super baker was known far and wide. Most people called her the Pie Lady. I helped Mama on weekends or when I wasn't in school, so folk started calling me Li'l' Pie. And a few people still call me Pie to this day.

It was an ordinary Tuesday morning when Pete Bruce stepped off the bus. Hot! My goodness, it was hot as blue blazes. Yet I noticed that this man had on a suit, fresh and crisp as if he'd just taken it off a cleaning rack. "How come he looks so neat when everybody else looks like they slept a week in their clothes?" I wondered out loud.

"A sign of good material," said Mama, who was studying the stranger as a potential customer.

We watched as he dabbed his brow with a perfectly folded white linen handkerchief. He checked the crease in his hat and placed it squarely on his head. Then he studied the surroundings, as if testing the wind, getting the lay of the land. Spying Mama and me, he picked up his carpetbag and started on over.

The man had an ageless body. By the bounce in his step, he could have been twenty, but the set of his brow told the story of a much older man. "Morning," he spoke real polite-like, flashing the biggest grin. "Name's Pete Bruce. Them coconut cream pies?" he asked Mama, examining the display she had arranged on the hood of our '28 Ford.

"Welcome to Masonville," Mama said cheerfully. "This is my daughter, Martha June. And yes, sir, these are coconut cream pies made by none other than Frenchie Mae Bosley, yours truly." Mama extended her hand and Pete Bruce took it and pumped it like a bellows. He grabbed mine and shook it, too, and I noticed how soft his was. This was not a man used to hard work.

"Pies do look good," he said, still holding that grin like an egg-stealing fox.

"Here, have a piece." Mama always let people taste a sliver of her sample pie. It was great for business, 'cause not one person had ever taken a taste and not bought a whole one. Sometimes they bought two.

Pete removed his hat—the way a man does when entering a church or a funeral—and clutched it to his chest. "No, ma'am," he said ever so courteously.

"What's the matter?" Mama said, sounding sympathetic. "You got sugar?"

He shook his head, lowered his eyes, and leaned on one foot and then the other. "No, ma'am, I aine diabetic." He sighed heavily.

"Well, what, then?" Mama was curious now.

"I mean no disrespect, Miz Frenchie, but there's a lady over in Steelville, Miz Opal Mary, she bakes the best cream pies in the world. Ummmm!" He closed his eyes as if eating one right then. "I—I have no doubt that your pie is delicious, but it just *can't* be as good as Miz Opal Mary's."

Mama's back stiffened. "How can you say that without having eaten mine?" she replied curtly.

Pete Bruce went back to shifting his weight from one foot to the other, eyes cast downward. "I'm sure your pies are fine, ma'am. But I'd rather not disappoint the last memory I have of Miz Opal Mary's rich, creamy, oh-so-sweet coconut cream pie."

Mama was beside herself. "I assure you, young man, there is no way in the world you would be disappointed if you ate a slice of *my* pie."

"I can't be sure," Pete said, looking like it made him sad to say it.

Quickly Mama cut a small wedge from her sample pie. She shoved it at Pete Bruce. Slowly, as if it pained him to do so, he put the whole thing in his mouth and chewed on it with his eyes closed. "Ummm," he moaned.

"Well, sir," said Mama confidently, "tell me the truth. Wasn't that the best thing you ever put in your mouth?"

Pete Bruce opened his eyes and shook his head. "I wish I could say, but . . ."

"But what?"

Pete shrugged. "I'm confused. It's hard to tell whose is better. Yours? Or Miz Opal Mary's?"

"I 'spect," said Mama, "yo' taste buds are mighty confused if you can't tell the difference 'tween my pie and that other what's-her-name." Mama cut an even larger piece; then, offering Pete a seat on the running board of her car, she handed it to him. She watched him bite into the creamy filling and flaky crust and chew it slowly.

"Mama," I whispered, trying to warn her. "You're not going to let him get away with—"

"Hush," Mama said, dismissing me with a wave.

Pete Bruce swallowed and smacked his lips. "Well," he said, licking his fingers, "I must say, Miz Frenchie, that was mighty good. But—"

"Don't say it. Don't you say it!" Mama held up a warning hand. She seemed almost desperate. "Here, have one more slice." Then she reached inside her apron for some money and sent me over to the store to get a pint of milk.

"Mama!" I tried to protest, but she shot me a look that said *You'd better do it or else.* So I did.

As I headed toward the grocery store, I heard Mama say, "A little milk will bring out the flavor," immediately adding, "not that my pie needs any help."

Soon as I was back, Mama shoved another huge slice at Pete

Bruce, along with the whole bottle of milk. He polished it all off in no time flat. Then Pete gave Mama one of those special smiles. "Ma'am, I do believe you got Miz Opal Mary beat by a country mile."

Mama's face lit up like a sunbeam. I hadn't seen her so happy since Li'l' Junior won the spelling bee the year before. Pete kissed the back of her hand, like a real fine gentleman in the movies—and I think Mama actually giggled. Once again Frenchie Mae Bosley was the undisputed best coconut cream pie baker in the county.

Pete Bruce popped a toothpick in his mouth, slung his carpet-bag over his shoulder, and started away. Turning back, he smiled at me, tipped his hat, and winked. In that instant I knew that he knew he hadn't fooled *me* one bit.

The rascal turned out to be one of Mama's best customers, and later on, when Mama passed and I opened my bakery, he became *my* best customer.

Pete Bruce!

Nothing but an ol' confidencer. Yes he was.

But he could always make me smile—in spite of myself. Yes he could.

CHANGE

Mr. Jesse Primo was a Universal Life Insurance *agent and a wonderful storyteller. Whenever he came to North Nashville to collect premiums, he made our house his last stop for the day. Mama Frances's sister, Aunt Will, had taught Mr. Primo at Tennessee State before it was a university. They loved to reminisce about another time and place.*

During one such visit, Mama Frances told Mr. Primo that all she had to pay her one-dollar premium with was a hundred-dollar bill. She asked if he could make ninety-nine dollars in change. Immediately Mr. Primo started laughing. Tears rolled down his cheeks and his whole body shook with wave after wave of laughter.

We didn't know what had overtaken Mr. Primo, who was usually as pressed and proper as his dark suit, conservative tie, and crisp white shirt.

At last he regained control, and he apologized, saying, "I'm sorry. There's an explanation for my outburst. Do you remember Mingo Cass?"

My grandmother's back stiffened. "Yes! But what does that rascal have to do with me?"

"Please," he said, sputtering into laughter again. "Let me share a story."

I found a comfortable seat where I could hear everything. Mr. Primo smiled, wiped a laugh tear from his eye, took a deep breath, and began one of the best porch lies I ever heard. "I knew Mingo Cass, too. . . ."

I started shining shoes at Benny's Barbershop on Murray Street, back in nineteen and thirty-four, when I was ten, eleven years old. There were a lot of regulars who hung around the place, but Mingo Cass was my favorite. When Mingo came in, he let me put a shine on his number eleven Stacy Adamses, all the while telling me stories about the time he spent in the rodeo, roping dogies in far-off places like Kansas City and Denver. Some say the stories were true; some say they were no more than porch lies.

I didn't care; I liked Mingo's style. He was a big man, brown-skinned, wide-shouldered; stood solid on his feet. I remember he had fists that looked like hammers. Wore his clothes well, always clean and polished from head to toe. No stink on him—nowhere at no time.

Mingo was quick to admit that he'd had to live by his wits. "Sure, I've had to make it best I could in this ol' world," he'd say, "but I never took nothing from nobody who didn't deserve it."

From where I sat that seemed true. Take my boss, Benny Foster, who owned the barbershop. Let him tell it, Mingo clipped him. But

Porch Lies

I was there and saw it all. And if you ask me, Benny got what was coming to him.

It all started one day when four or five regulars were in Benny's shop, conversating 'bout Mingo Cass. Benny, who come from one of them sea islands off the South Carolina coast, talked right fast, running his words together, saying things like "day-clean" for early morning and such.

"That rascal Mingo Cass can snatch de sugar out of cake an' convince e'r'body that cake's s'*posed* to be bitter," Benny say.

"Yeah, yeah, yeah, he's a slickster, a'right," agreed Wallace Maywood, one of the shop flies. "I hate to tell this on myself, but Mingo bet me fifty cents that it was raining. Now, I was looking at the sun shining, so I took the bet."

Everybody commenced to laughing, 'cause they'd already heard the story.

Wallace went on. "That's when Mingo turned to a newspaper article 'bout a raging hurricane in Florida. It was raining cats and dogs *there*, he told me. I went to arguing that I thought he meant it was raining right *here* in Masonville. Course, he threw them cold, hawkish-looking eyes on me, and say—he say, 'Wall'—that's what he calls me—'Wall, why would I bet you that it was raining *here*, when we both can see the sun shining?' Then Mingo slaps me on the back and adds, 'Did you really think I'd be that dumb?'

" 'No . . . well, yes . . . I mean no . . . ,' I sputtered. Fact is, I didn't know what to say. So I just shut up and paid up."

There were rounds of thigh slapping and hee-hawing all around the place. I wasn't sure if Wallace's buddies were laughing with him or at him. No matter, it was a funny story. And I laughed, too.

None of it was funny to Wallace. "Do you realize how hard fifty cents is to come by these days?" he asked.

"I sure do," I put in. "I'd have to shine five pairs of shoes to make that kind of money."

Sam Perkins took the floor next. He hitched up his pants, then clicked his teeth. "Mingo Cass got me once." He took a toothpick out of his mouth and commenced to using it as a pointer. "We both had part-time work over at the quarry. One day round noon-thirty, Mingo suggested we eat lunch together. I shoulda knowed better, but I dropped my guard. Since Mingo was driving, I jumped out and bought two meat loaf sandwiches and two soda pops down at Sadie's Place. Paid for both, figuring we'd square up later. Mingo drove us over to the bluffs, and we watched the river traffic go by whilst we ate.

"After we finished, I says, 'The sandwich was fifteen cents, and a nickel for the soda pop.' Mingo dug round in his pockets. 'Man,' he says, 'I thought I had . . . Hey, all I got is a hundred-dollar bill. You got change?'

" 'One hundred dollars! Aine you heard?' I shouted. 'There's a depression going on. Mingo, how many folk do you know walking round with change for a hundred dollars in they pockets?'

"Mingo shrugged and says real matter-of-fact-like, 'Sorry, Perk. I'll have to catch you next time, then. Okay?' And before I could say a word Mingo was gone. And so was my twenty cents."

"He got me for a quart of oil using that same line," said Jackson Perry, the local filling station attendant. "Boss took it out of my paycheck." Just then Jackson got an idea and bolted right out of his chair. "Hey! Do you reckon Mingo's really got a hundred-dollar bill?"

Benny stomped his foot. "No! And if we don't stop him, that Mingo Cass will nickel-and-dime us all the way to the po'house." Plenty of nods went around.

From then on, they took turns scandalizing Mingo in a terrible way. Nobody had a kind word to say about him. I couldn't take it anymore, so I spoke up. "Mr. Cass aine all that bad."

"Jus' wait, Jesse. He aine got to you yet," Jackson scoffed.

"Keep living," Sam added.

"And if he don't get you here on earth, he'll be at the Pearly Gates selling sunglasses to shade yo' eyes from the glow of the heavenly throne," Benny say, followed by another round of laughter.

Just then, who stepped through the door like a fresh breeze? None other than Mingo Cass himself. The temperature dropped ten degrees. Everything fell quiet. All you could hear was Benny's scissors going *snip, snip, snip,* and *snip.* Sam went to picking at invisible lint on his clothes. Jackson pulled his ears, and Wallace tapped his fingers on the arm of his chair.

Nobody said a word. Mingo studied their faces; then he broke into a full grin. "Aha! Musta caught y'all talkin' 'bout me. Right?"

Everybody went to chattering at once, denying they'd given him a thought—hadn't let his name cross their lips. Mingo kept on laughing.

"Howdy, Mr. Cass. Shoeshine today?" I asked.

"Sounds good to me, Jesse. Make 'em mirrors." He took a seat.

I went to work laying on the bootblack, then brushed each shoe until it was even and shiny. Next, I took out my smoothing rag and make it zing and zap until those shoes were patent-leather glossy. The whole time Mingo was studying the mood of the barbershop.

"Ten cents, Mr. Cass," I said when I'd finished.

Mingo dug around in his pockets. "Man, oh, man," he said, sighing. "All I have is a hundred-dollar bill, kid, and I know you can't make change. Let me catch you later, okay?"

Benny threw up his arms and started sputtering that real fast Geechie talk. "You done sunk to the bottom-low," he shouted at Mingo, breathless with emotion. "Trying to con Jesse, a po' hard-working boy, out of a ten-cent shoeshine! Shame on you!"

I quickly put in, "No trouble, Mr. Cass. You can bring me the money later."

But Benny wouldn't leave it alone. "Mingo! You—you—you been using that hundred-dollar bill to bamboozle us way too long."

Mingo looked surprised. "What's got you all hot and bothered and rumbling like a empty freight train? I don't have change." He shrugged. "Why do I have to be a bamboozler because I aine got change?"

Benny stopped cutting hair. He stepped from behind his chair and stood toe to toe with Mingo. "I don't b'lieve you got no hundred-dollar bill."

The entire barbershop crowd nodded in agreement. Benny had thrown down the gauntlet. Mingo had been called out.

"Show us the money," Jackson said boldly.

With a little encouragement, Benny rushed on. "Guess what, Mr. Hundred-Dollar Bill? I got change for you right here in my cash register. So let's see the money. Now."

They reminded me of a wolf pack, circling their prey, sizing him up, ready to pounce at the first sign of weakness.

But Mingo Cass stood his ground. His head was slightly tilted as he eyed his accusers with a look of disappointment. "Hey, look," he said, holding up his hands and stepping back to put space between him and Benny. "I didn't come in here to cause confusion. I'll just leave and bring *Jesse* back *his* money some other time."

But the men wouldn't let him leave.

Benny positioned himself between Mingo and the door. He was so sure of himself, he pointed his finger at the man. "I bet you a year of free haircuts that you aine got nothing that looks like a hundred-dollar bill in yo' wallet," he shouted.

That's when Mingo's whole persona changed. The humble and conciliatory posture evaporated. Though he was still smiling, his eyes changed to those of a predator. If Benny had been observant, he would have seen that he was now the prey.

"I'll take the bet," Mingo said, as cool as springwater. "And I'll bet any of you fellas that want in on it. Just remember, this was all *your* idea."

The others couldn't wait to get a piece of the action. I watched openmouthed as each and every last man laid his hard-earned nickels, dimes, and quarters against Mingo Cass.

As for me, I passed. And when all the bets were set, there must have been two weeks' salary on the table, plus a year of free haircuts.

Mingo asked once again, "Y'all sure you want to do this?"

"Stop stalling," Benny said impatiently. "Show us the hundred-dollar bill . . . that you aine got!" And they all laughed again.

To everyone's surprise (but mine), Mingo dropped his head and walked to the door, saying, "I don't want to do this to y'all. I like you, even though you question my honesty. Trust me, I have my money. Don't throw yours away." He opened the door and the bells jangled.

"See, told you!" Benny roared with laughter. "See, he aine got it. Aine got it!" They all started slapping shoulders and stomping their feet with excitement.

The bells jangled again when Mingo closed the door and walked back to the center of the shop. He held up his hands to silence the jeering. "Okay. Okay. Since you insist."

He took out his wallet. "It's in here somewhere," he said, searching the compartments. "I just saw it. . . ."

You coulda heard an ant crawling on cotton when Mingo paused and sighed. "Here we go," he said, finally producing a crisp hundred-dollar bill. He kissed it and held it up for everybody to see.

Benny fell back in his barber's chair, dumbstruck. Jackson repeatedly slapped the heel of his hand into his forehead and eyed the money as though he was looking at the crown jewels of England.

"I aine never seen a hundred-dollar bill before," said Wallace. "Is it real?"

That gave Benny a ray of hope. He snatched up the bill and held it to the light, trying to find some sign that it might be fake. But it was real, all right, and the barber dropped his head in defeat.

Still smiling, Mingo picked up his winnings, then declared, "Well, sir, looks like I don't need change after all." And he laid thirty cents in Sam's outstretched hand, saying, "Lunch paid for with interest."

Ten cents, twenty cents, a quarter. He went around that barbershop paying every man the money he was owed. Then, looking at

Benny, he chuckled, "I'll be in on the first Tuesday of every month for my *free* haircuts."

Before turning on his heels to go, Mingo flipped a quarter to me. "We all square now?"

I nodded, too amazed to speak.

Mingo placed the rest of his winnings and the hundred-dollar bill neatly in his wallet. Heading toward the door, he called over his shoulder, "Maybe one day I'll get this bill changed. Having it can be downright inconvenient sometimes.

"Or then again, maybe I won't."

THE DEVIL'S GUITAR

Dedicated to Ron Hines and my friends at the St. Louis Black Rep, who are successful without playing the Devil's guitar

Mr. James "Bukka" Black was the band director at T. Thomas Hutchinson High School. It was said all over town that Mr. Black could have been the greatest blues guitar man there ever was, bar none—not even the renowned Robert Johnson. But he chose to be a teacher instead.

Even so, Mr. Black could brag that he had the best high school music program in the state, and he could back up his brag with the fact that his marching band had won five national trophies.

Everybody wanted to be a member of Mr. Black's band, but he didn't accept just anybody. Off the field, he insisted that his band members attend all classes, maintain respectable grades, and be of good character. He didn't put up with any foolishness. On the field, he expected all band members to be on time for practice, to be responsible, and to reach for the stars. "As humans we can never achieve perfection, but we can try to be as good as we can be," he told all incoming freshmen.

My neighbor Bobby thought Mr. Black was too strict and his rules too rigid, so he quit the band.

A day or two later, Mr. Black visited my house, and Bobby just happened to be there. (Later I found out Mama Frances and Bobby's mama had planned the "chance" meeting.) Mr. Black took a seat on the glider. "Good to see you, Bobby," he said. They exchanged a few pleasantries; then Mr. Black said, "I'd like to share a little piece of my life with you. You willing to listen?"

Bobby nodded.

By the time Mr. Black finished, my friend had a different opinion of Mr. Black. To everyone's joy, Bobby rejoined the band. This, then, is the story Mr. Black told us. You decide if it's a porch lie or not.

My name is James Booker Black, but everybody in my family has always called me Bukka. When I was twelve years old, I slipped under the crawl space of Sukie's Juke Joint to hear Robert Johnson play the blues guitar, and from that day on I was determined to follow in the great man's footsteps.

I picked cotton, peaches, and peas to earn enough money to buy a $19.99 guitar from a Sears and Roebuck catalog. Didn't matter to me that it was the cheapest one in the book. I cherished that guitar, and taught myself how to play it. In a few years I got so good at strumming, Sukie invited me to play at her annual barbecue over at Okashone Lake. After that, things started happening. I got a gig in Selma playing at the Elks Club, and I worked a wedding in Barbee Flats.

Porch Lies

By the beginning of summer, Sonny Pike, the leader of a blues quartet, heard me at a Livingston wedding. Sonny asked me to replace his guitarist, who'd just quit. I agreed—you bet I did!

Since I was underage, I needed to get permission from my mama; then I was supposed to catch up with Sonny and the group in Jackson, Mississippi, the following week.

But Mama wouldn't sign for me to go.

She was dead set against me joining a blues quartet, never mind playing honky-tonk music on tour. "You know the story of the prodigal son," she fretted. "It's easy to be dazzled by the bright lights of the sin-filled cities of Babylon."

"Mama, I'm not going to Babylon. I'm going to Jackson, and that aine a hundred miles away."

"I'm just afraid you'll get in with the wrong crowd."

I hugged Mama, trying to console her troubled mind. "I don't need to go miles away to do something wrong."

"I was just hoping you'd maybe think about going to Tuskegee Institute. Getting a college education. Really doing something with your talent."

I felt like I was doing fine with my talent. Besides, I wanted to be famous. I wanted to be rich, drive fancy cars, and live in a mansion—even buy Mama a grand house and new Sunday dresses, one for every week in the year. "I'm a good musician now," I said. "Why do I need to waste time in school when I could be on my way to fame and fortune?"

"What do you know? You're not yet eighteen years old."

"Robert Johnson was younger than me when he began his career."

Mama fell back in her chair and sighed deeply. "Oh, son of mine! Don't you know 'bout Robert Johnson?" She looked more worried than before.

I started packing while she continued. "That Johnson man you wanting to be like, word is he would've done anything to be rich and famous. It caught the Devil's attention, and he visited that blues guitar player at the Crossroads. They tell me the Devil offered Robert Johnson a guitar that would guarantee him success, but the cost of it was to be Johnson's soul. Rumor is that the Devil's planning to collect one of these days soon. Remember, the Devil don't give you nothing without coming to get his pay."

"Mama! You don't believe that Crossroads tale, do you?" I asked, shaking my head in disbelief. I had finished packing and was heading for the door. "Sign the permission paper so I can be on my way, please."

Mama blocked the exit with outstretched arms. "You're underage. I could stop you."

In those days, I was stubborn and haughty, and that made me bold enough to speak harshly to my mother. "You can stop me for a few months, but when I turn eighteen, I'm gone. And there won't be anything you can do about it. So it's now or a little bit later—whatever you want."

Mama dropped her arms and sighed deeply. "I reckon you've made up yo' mind. But just remember, when yo' senses return, come on back home." She wept silently as she signed the permission paper.

"I'll be home so soon you won't have time to miss me," I said, hurrying away before she could change her mind.

Porch Lies

✖✖✖✖

All through the summer I played with Sonny Pike's group. The guys were ten or fifteen years older than I was, but I fit in well. Sonny was on piano and sang lead. Jake was on drums. Larry played bass, and I was on guitar. We were good, if I do say so.

Others thought we were good, too. We drew big crowds at dances, picnics, birthday parties, and the like.

Before I knew it summer was over. I was enjoying myself way too much to think about going home, so I wrote Mama and told her I'd be back for Christmas. That was my honest intention.

Meanwhile, I turned eighteen and we started on the honky-tonk circuit, never staying more than two or three nights in one place. Back then, times were bad for everybody, but especially for an all-black group in the South. After we shared the applause onstage, we often split a bologna sandwich and slept in Sonny's Ford. Most hotels and restaurants weren't open to blacks back in nineteen and thirty-four.

Even so, I was happy. I enjoyed listening to the older guys tell one story after another about places they'd been and people they'd met. A favorite was one Sonny told about the Alabama sheriff who pulled them over and accused them of stealing their instruments.

"We're musicians," Sonny had told the sheriff. "Honest to goodness, truly, we are musicians, sir."

"Well, ya gon' have to prove it to me," the sheriff said. "Play me a song."

"So there we were," said Sonny, laughing until his eyes ran

water, "playing a gig for the sheriff at one o'clock a.m. on the side of an Alabama road with a cotton field as our stage curtain."

"That's the closest we've ever gotten to playing at the Cotton Club," Jake chuckled.

"Did the sheriff enjoy the show?" I asked.

"He must have, 'cause he let us go," said Larry.

I loved their friendship, but I was happiest onstage strumming my guitar. When I wasn't playing for work, I played just for fun. And I was getting better and better. Sonny began giving me solos and allowing me to sing more, too. Soon I was getting requests from the customers—especially the young ladies. After we played at a little hole in the wall outside of Knoxville, a girl who was about the prettiest thing I'd ever seen came running up to me with sparkling eyes. She asked, "Are you a big-time recording star?"

"No, miss, not yet," I said.

The light went out in that girl's eyes when I told her my name and that I wasn't really famous. And I promised myself right then and there, *One day girls will look at me—Bukka Black—with starlight in their eyes.*

In another town on the outskirts of Macon, a cute little Georgia peach gave me a big smile and said, "You are the best bluesman I've ever heard."

"Did you hear that?" I asked the others, with my shoulders pulled back.

"I reckon she aine heard much," said Jake, with that same devilish chuckle. Then he added, "Boy, don't you know you can't b'lieve everything a honky-tonk woman tells you?"

"You got to *live the blues* before you can even compete for the title of *best*," Sonny put in. "You aine stood at the Crossroads. And until you do, you'll be a good player, maybe even very good, but you won't be counted among the best—not till you've experienced some of life's highs and lows. Hear me when I'm talking, boy."

But I paid them no mind. I kept on dreaming, and in my spare time I practiced and practiced, really put my back into it. I would be the best—soon.

One evening we were working a dance in Jacksonville, Florida. Somebody said there was a recording agent in the audience. I figured this was my chance. I had to get noticed, stand out from the others.

So even before it was my time to solo, I tried something new— a combination of tricky chords to dazzle the crowd. Trouble is, I hadn't rehearsed with Sonny and the group. They got lost, and we ended up sounding so awful, all the customers booed and walked out—including the big-time recording agent. Worse still, the owner refused to pay Sonny. When Sonny wouldn't take no for an answer, two big bouncers came over and threw us out.

I'd caused a grand mess, so I sat very still and tried to make myself as small as possible as we rode away. Sonny was so mad I could smell the anger rising off him like steam off a boiling pot. He didn't speak a word until we were almost to Brunswick. Out there in the middle of nowhere he stopped the car.

We all rolled out, one behind the other. I was the last. Sonny stood nose to nose with me. "Listen careful-like, Bukka, 'cause we aine gon' have this conversation no mo'. Do you want to play *with* me?"

I nodded.

Sonny went on as if my answer didn't matter. "Don't you ever, *ev*-er play something we aine rehearsed. If you want to showboat, then become a solo act. It won't upset me any. But you can't mess up my stuff like you did tonight."

Then Sonny slid back into the driver's seat. "Don't ever do that again, boy, never in life! Do you understand?"

I understood.

From then on, I stuck with what we practiced. Fame and fortune had to wait.

The four of us worked together through Christmas without a cross word between us. I missed Mama something awful during the holidays, but it was our busiest time. As soon as my fingers touched the strings on my guitar, I forgot my pain. *I'll go home, come spring,* I promised myself, and sent Mama a card with five dollars and a note inside saying, "Buy something pretty for somebody sweet."

"You've lasted longer than we thought," Sonny said to me one day in early March. "We thought you woulda run back home a long time ago."

I shook my head. Naw. I wasn't famous yet. I wasn't rich yet. "If I can't drive up in front of my mama's house in a brand-new car, then I don't want to go home," I explained.

And I didn't. Spring came. Many a stormy Monday passed and I crossed over a lot of muddy waters. Still I didn't go home.

Days seemed to flip over like the pages of a book, and before I knew it a full year had gone by. It was about that time that a producer at Decca Records offered Sonny a contract to cut a single. Naturally, he jumped at the opportunity, even though it meant the group had to split up. I was happy for him, because the way I figured, if Sonny could make it, then maybe so could I.

"You deserve it, Sonny," said Jake.

"Better one of us than none of us," Larry said good-naturedly.

"You're in the driver's seat now," I added.

After our last gig together in Louisiana, in late September, we all shook hands.

"I think I'll head for California," said Larry. "They might need a good-looking man like me to star in one of those Hollywood pictures."

We all laughed. "What you gon' do?" I asked Jake.

"I think I'll go on up to Detroit. Hear they're hiring at the auto plant. Get me a real job, a good woman, settle down. I'm sick of the road."

"What about you, kid?" Sonny asked.

"I'm gon' play on my own. See if a recording contract comes my way."

Sonny smiled. "You still looking for fame and fortune?" he asked.

"More than ever."

"Hang in there, then," Sonny said, patting me on the back. "You're good enough, but take a fool's advice: be patient with the blues. It took me twenty years to know the blues well enough to play 'em. But I never sold my soul. You can make it without selling your soul, too. Don't grab for the Devil's guitar."

I thanked him, but I remember thinking at the time: *I'd play anybody's guitar as long as it got me a recording contract. And it wouldn't take twenty years to do it, either.*

Meanwhile, I wrote Mama; told her I would be gone a little longer than expected.

It was the height of the Depression. When times are bad and people are out of work, they often turn to music—especially the blues—to express their frustrations, anger, fear, and pain. Good blues musicians were in demand. All I needed was a break, and I was sure my success was right around the corner just waiting to run into me.

But as fall pressed on, I never got that break. "You have a good sound, kid, but you aine quite there," said one promoter after the other.

"Your music is too tame for my place," said one owner.

"Your style is too wild for my clientele," said another.

Nothing I did seemed to work. So I practiced longer and harder, only to hear the same thing. "You're good, son, but you just aine good enough."

What was good enough? Nobody, it seemed, could tell me.

Without work, I was soon broke. Sonny had managed all the money for the quartet, and I'd always had a buck or two. I didn't know the first thing about managing on my own, so I ended up penniless, hungry, and with no place to lay my head.

One night as I sat on the side of a Tennessee road, a raindrop splattered on my forehead. I thought, *I should get home 'fore the storm comes.* Then it struck me like a ton of bricks: my home was far, far away. "You can always come back" is what Mama had told me. So I decided maybe it was time to head that way . . . at least for a visit.

Porch Lies

In my mother's house I could sleep in a clean bed and eat well-prepared food—greens, sweet potatoes, okra, and corn bread. Home. Sounded perfect to me. That was where I wanted to be.

Trouble was, I didn't have two nickels to rub together to buy a bus ticket, and I was too proud to ask Mama to send me money. So, with my guitar slung over my shoulder, and toting the same beat-up carpetbag I'd left town with, I started walking toward Clayton, Alabama. Home.

After ten miles, give or take a few, I was tired and thirsty, so I stopped by a little joint just over the Mississippi state line outside of Memphis. "Aine got a dime," I told the waitress, "but I'll play you a song for a glass of cold water."

"What makes you think I'd want to hear any song you got to play?" she asked smartly.

I took out my guitar and hit a few familiar chords.

"Oh my goodness," she said with a big smile on her face. "You're Robert Johnson."

I was about to deny it, but when I looked at her sparkling eyes, I remembered the way that girl had looked at me in Knoxville. I couldn't bring myself to tell her that I was just plain ol' Bukka Black.

The girl ran to find her daddy, who owned the place. "He's here! Right here!" she said breathlessly, all the time leading an elderly gent out of the kitchen.

"Mr. Johnson, I'm Willie Jenkins," said the man, extending his hand and smiling broadly. "And I'm real happy you're in my place of establishment. You take a seat over there by the window and we'll be serving you the house special . . . right over there. Yes indeed."

Before I knew it, the little place was full of onlookers, all come to get a glimpse of the famous Robert Johnson. It wasn't my intention to deceive them. But if they wanted Robert Johnson, I could give him to them.

And simple as that, one minute I was Bukka Black, a nobody, and the next minute I was Robert Johnson, famous blues guitarist and recording star.

Later that evening I played a gig at the local Elks Club as Robert Johnson, swearing to myself that the next time I'd let people know who I really was, for sure. But instead I accepted an offer to play a big club just off the highway . . . as Robert Johnson.

It wasn't hard to make the transition. We looked enough alike to be brothers, and I'd already studied the bluesman like a doctor. Now I listened to Robert Johnson's records over and over, learning the words to his songs and copying his every strum. I changed my hair to look more like his and I wore the same cut of brightly colored suits and flip-flop hats. I tried to walk like him, sorta leading with my left shoulder. My impersonation was so complete nobody once questioned my authenticity.

Still, it felt like I was walking a tightrope. I was careful not to say I actually *was* Robert Johnson. Never said I wasn't, either. Didn't have to say much of anything. As soon as I began playing, people told me who I was.

I was so convincing that once when the real Robert Johnson showed up in Waycross, Georgia, a few days after I had played, the crowd forced him off the stage, calling *him* an impersonator. "I've been accused of a lot, but I've never been accused of not being myself," Johnson was heard to say as he fled the stage.

Within months my life made a complete turnaround. I didn't have great wealth, but I had enough money to send home for Mama to put away. Women adored me. Men envied me. Club owners welcomed me. I was on the way to getting everything I'd ever wanted, but I felt empty—sad and lonely. My success was all based on a lie. I told myself it was my talent that made the deception work. But I also knew that the moment I took off the disguise and let people know who I really was—plain ol' Bukka Black—the party would be over.

So I held on to the falsehood like a lifeline. And for a year and two days, I ran the circuit as Robert Johnson. Then one night I caught the attention of someone to whom Johnson owed a tremendous debt.

I was playing in a little place over in Savannah, Georgia, when the clock struck midnight—hag hollering time, according to the locals. The doors swung open and a gush of hot smoky air filled the room. From out of the haze there appeared a stranger who was as mysterious as he was sharply dressed. He had on a fine cut of clothes, starched shirt, silk tie, soft leather shoes, diamond cuff links and a tie tack to match. Beside him stood a blue-black hellhound with cinder red eyes.

"Sit," the stranger said, and the huge dog obeyed without pause. "Stay."

"I'm here for Robert Johnson," the stranger announced, sounding like a hundred voices speaking at once.

Everybody knew the intruder was the Devil himself, no doubt

come at last to collect the soul of Robert Johnson as final payment for use of his guitar. *So what Mama said was true,* I thought as the bartender pointed in my direction.

"Th—that's him over there, sir," he said, trembling.

Folk commenced to running over each other, knocking against chairs and pulling hair, trying to get out of that hole-in-the-wall.

The Devil watched those lost souls scampering like mice fleeing a cat attack. "Run now, but I'll see you all in due time," he said, laughing—a gleeful squeal of delight that trailed off and became a dark and sinister howl.

I wanted to run, too, but the hellhound blocked my way.

"Robert Johnson. It's time to collect on the debt you owe me," said the Devil.

"Naw, sir," I said softly, so as not to rile him. "I aine really John son. I'm Bukka Black from Clayton, Alabama. Can't you see, I don't look nothing like Robert Johnson."

"Peel away the skin and you mortals all look the same to me," said the Devil. "Besides, people change how they look all the time, thinking they can fool me!" Then he smiled wickedly. "But I have ways of knowing who people really are. I'd know the sound of my guitar anywhere, Robert Johnson!" He pointed at me and my insides quivered.

Desperately I tried to think of some way to save myself. "You gave Robert Johnson his guitar, right?" My voice was real unsteady-like.

"I did."

"He never, ever lets anybody play it—or even touch it, right?"

"What's your point?" The Devil was getting impatient.

Porch Lies

I handed my guitar to the Devil. "Here's what I play. Cheap as rainwater. Bought it out of a catalog for nineteen ninety-nine. It's the only guitar I've ever owned. Would the real Robert Johnson play this thing?"

The Devil didn't answer. He pushed the guitar away as if it was something stinking. "Play," he ordered.

I played a simple little ditty that a beginner might pick. The Devil blew up a storm inside the small tavern. "I said play a *song*. Don't make me ask you again, mortal!"

My knees were shaking and I could hardly breathe, but I struck up a tune. The Devil closed his eyes. "Ha, ha! I'd know that sound anywhere. You can't fool me, Bobby Boy."

I got scared then for sure. All my life I had wanted to be somebody great. Now all I wanted was to be plain old Bukka Black from Clayton, Alabama.

Without even planning it, I began to sing my life. I moaned and groaned 'bout my mama and how much I had hurt her by leaving home. I wailed 'bout how I'd done wrong just for attention and glory, but I was sorry, truly sorry. If I had another chance I'd do much better, I would.

All the time I was singing, I was strumming that cheap little guitar. Every note was a stretch; every chord was original. The music came tumbling out of me, filling the room with my own sound—not music I was imitating or stealing; not a song I played to make money or to be well-known. My fingers found new chords and fresh combinations that came from my core. This was the real Bukka Black playing the blues!

When I finished, my body was soaking wet and my legs were

weak as water. The Devil was speechless, and even the hellhound flopped down beside me and sighed.

"Well, well, well," said the Devil, kicking his dog. He took the guitar from my hands. "I'm impressed." He examined my catalog instrument. "You got all that sound out of this cheap little thing?"

I nodded.

He smiled and raised an eyebrow. "Well, you're right. This aine my instrument. Fact is, I don't know who you are, but I suppose you aine Robert Johnson."

I was relieved, but it was too soon. The Devil saw an opportunity before him and he wasn't about to pass it up. He slid up beside me and put his arm on my shoulder like a loving friend. And in a sure voice, he whispered, "You've got talent, boy. But think of how much better you'd be if you played one of *my* guitars."

He snapped his fingers. "Come, Lovey," he called over his shoulder, the way one calls a servant.

Out of the haze stepped a brown-skinned beauty with familiar sparkling eyes. She was carrying a guitar case with a hexagram on the top. I watched as she sashayed up to the Devil and presented it to him as if it was a gift. She winked at me, and even though I didn't want to, I blushed. It didn't go unnoticed by the Devil.

Dramatically, the Devil opened the case and took out the most beautiful guitar I'd ever seen. As knock-you-down pretty as Lovey was, I couldn't take my eyes off that instrument. The Devil handed it to me, knowing all the while what I was thinking. I embraced it with my fingers. It was a far cry from the cheap thing I'd been playing. *What could I do with this in my hands?* I wondered.

"Go on, play something. Get the feel of it," said Lovey sweetly.

I tried a few chords and soon a song was forming. Just as I'd thought, the marriage of fingers and strings was producing wonderful creations. The new music filled the room and lifted me out of my chair. The Devil's guitar was truly magical!

As the Devil's hellhound howled, Lovey swooned and swayed to the beat—*my* beat—all the time encouraging me to play more. The Devil read my every thought and gave Lovey words to say. They were pretty words, flattering words, charm-filled words. "You'll be famous," she whispered. "More famous than Robert Johnson ever was or will be. You can have it all . . . and me, too."

"And with her on your arm, you'll be the envy of every man who sees you. Play *my* guitar, Bukka Black. You deserve it."

As I played, an image suddenly formed in my head. It was of Mama. She was praying. I blinked and her picture was replaced by Sonny, warning me to stay away from the Devil's guitar. I closed my eyes and tried to push the images away, but my past would not leave me alone.

My playing slowed then, and I sighed deeply. The magic of the guitar seemed to be wearing off, and the music didn't sound the same.

I knew what I had to do. With a touch of regret, I placed the guitar in its case and closed the lid. "No, thank you," I said to the Devil.

Lovey's eyes turned green and she screamed like a wounded mountain lion. "You fool! How could you pass up such an offer?" Then both the guitar and Lovey vanished.

"Thank you kindly," I said to the Devil, not knowing what to expect. "But I'll trust my own talent to take me where I should go. I don't need the Devil's guitar."

The Devil was silent. When he finally spoke, his voice was surprisingly soft, but filled with controlled anger. "I'll tell you where all that righteous, sentimental stuff will lead you, Bukka Black." His voice exploded into a deafening rage. "Back to Clayton, Alabama!"

The Devil's eyes flashed flames and he hissed and sputtered as he ranted on. "Let me show you the picture of your pitiful life. You'll crawl back to yo' mama's house, go back to school, get a degree from Tuskegee, and teach music to unappreciative high school kids in Nashville, Tennessee, for the rest of your boring, insignificant little life!"

"Right now that doesn't sound so bad to me," I said, voice trembling.

"Disgusting!" scoffed the Devil. The room filled with smoke and the strong smell of sulfur. "I'm through with you . . . for now." Then everything fell quiet.

When I was sure the Prince of Darkness was gone, I let out a low whistle of relief. "Thank goodness," I said, setting out for Mama's house that very night.

AUNT GRAN AND THE OUTLAWS

Dedicated to my husband,
Fred, who gave me this
story

Papa Jack's porch lies were usually about *little girls who outsmarted foxes or captured the wind. But one evening he told me about growing up with his great-aunt, who lived in Webb Hollow, an all-black community on the Tennessee-Arkansas border.*

After supper Papa Jack found his favorite spot, then beckoned for me to sit beside him on the porch swing. "Tell me a story about back in the olden days," I asked.

He got the swing to swaying, then began. "Way back when I was no bigger than you, Webb Hollow was a thriving town. Then, after World War One, people moved away. . . . Better opportunities up north, so the little town died out. But my memories are of Webb Hollow back in its heyday.

"My great-aunt, Henrietta McClintock, raised me. She called me Junior, and since she was like an extra grandmother, I called her Aunt Gran. Truth be told, she became Aunt Gran to all who knew her,"

Porch Lies

Papa Jack explained, "including two of the most notorious outlaws in America."

I sucked in a mouthful of night air and leaned back against his arm. "How did Aunt Gran come to know outlaws?" I could feel a story coming.

"Let me see if I can put it together again," Papa Jack said, stroking his gray beard. "I was twelve. I'm eighty-two years old now, so it must have been eighteen and eighty-two when those two bandits came riding up the road. . . ."

It had been a bitter winter, one of the coldest in Tennessee memory. An outbreak of whooping cough took my little sister, Jenny, and many others. Then the spring rains flooded the fields and held off planting season for weeks. But the land had cottoned out anyway from overplanting, and it wouldn't even now grow a thistle. We were all hurting, but to add sorrow to suffering, the Knights of the White Gardenia were back.

The Knights were the worst gang of hate-filled Confederates ever there was. They'd organized after the war to stop us black folk from becoming citizens. They covered themselves in black hoods and rode through the Hollow, burning barns and scaring women and children.

Their first target was the small school Northern soldiers had built in eighteen and sixty-five and named the Union School for Colored Children. The Knights would not suffer it to stand—they torched it. But the citizens of Webb Hollow rebuilt, and renamed it George Washington School after the first president, hoping this would keep it safe. The Knights destroyed it again and then again.

After the little one-room shack of a school had been burned three times, the people lost heart and didn't bother to rebuild. So Webb Hollow had no school. The closest one was twenty-two miles away in Dyersburg.

For a while the Knights disbanded. Then, during the winter of 1882, Green Farley came to the Hollow. Farley was a private agent who represented a large paper mill over in Memphis. He was offering big contracts to white farmers for their timberland. But when he made offers to black farmers for our land, the amount of money was so small, it was little mor'n highway robbery. We black folk 'fused to sell . . . so the Knights began their midnight rides again. They thought they could scare us into giving up.

Green Farley was behind the attacks, a'right. He was a greedy man, determined to get his hands on what was rightfully ours and then sell it to the paper mill at a higher price.

Fearful for our families, some of us considered accepting his offer. But the idea of surrendering our land was painful. Most of the people who lived in Webb Hollow were former slaves who cherished the idea of freedom. Owning land was hard evidence of that freedom.

My aunt Gran encouraged us to stand our ground.

"Don't sell out," she said during a meeting at the African Methodist Episcopal church. "Our property is valuable to us in ways Farley will never be able to understand. We slaved on this land. Now we own a piece of it, not just for our use, but for our children's and their children's. No man is lord and master over us anymore. We can fight Farley."

Heads nodded in agreement.

"I aine disagreeing with you, Aunt Gran," put in Willie Watkins, "but fight Farley and the Knights with *what*? They're stronger than we are. They got guns, and the law aine gon' help."

Heads nodded his way now.

"What we need is a different kinda help. We need somebody who can stand toe to toe with them," argued Aunt Gran. "It's like my mama used to say—we need a wolf to chase off a fox."

"I see what you mean," said Abraham Simms, who was like our unofficial mayor. "Trouble is, what do we do with the wolf once he's run off the fox?"

"We'll cross that bridge if and when we come to it. Besides," Aunt Gran added, "we aine even now got the wolf yet."

Everybody laughed.

"All I ask is that you don't give up."

"We'll stand with you," said Jonas Neal. Others joined him, pledging their loyalty to the end.

Meanwhile, Farley and the Knights really put the pressure on. In the shadows of darkness, under black hoods, they burned our barns and poisoned our livestock.

The sheriff did nothing.

One bright morning, Farley came to Aunt Gran's house, hat in hand. Every word was honey coated. "You're one of the leaders in the community," he said with a foxy smile. "Why don't you and me become partners? You talk your people into selling their land to me, and I'll make it worth your while."

Aunt Gran snatched the door open. "Get thee behind me, Fallen Angel," she declared, and ushered him out of her house.

"You best watch what you say. You have no idea who you're tangling with," Farley fumed.

"If I was you, I'd be particular 'bout who you threaten. I've got Somebody on my side who watches over me."

"Ol' woman, who do you have watching over you that would dare challenge me?"

Aunt Gran slammed the door in his face. Seems Farley couldn't understand her simple statement of faith.

But Farley wasn't one to give up. The next day, our well went bad. We learned later that Farley and the Knights had hurled bags of salt into it, making the water undrinkable. They knew it was near impossible to farm without a source of fresh water.

They also knew it was tax time. We'd barely pieced together the tax money by raising and selling chickens, eggs, and butter and taking in laundry. I'd even made brooms and baskets and sold them, to earn my part. Now Aunt Gran had to make a tough choice: should she pay the taxes? Or should she pay to take care of the well? There wasn't enough money for both.

Farley may have figured he had Aunt Gran cornered. But he didn't know she wasn't one to scare easily—or to give up, either.

"Lawd, Lawd, Lawd," I heard Aunt Gran cry out in the night. "No need taking up too much of yo' time. Please, send somebody who can help. Thy will be done. Amen."

Early the next morning Aunt Gran said to me, "Junior, I'm going to pay the taxes. We'll just have to leave the well till later."

It really didn't matter. We were going to lose the farm regardless of what she did with the money. "Don't look so sad," Aunt Gran said, lifting my chin. "We'll make it." Then she went back to churning butter and singing one of her favorite spirituals.

> "Swing low, sweet chariot,
> Coming for to carry me home,
> Swing low, sweet chariot,
> Coming for to carry me home."

I was sweeping the yard when out of nowhere, two young white men wearing pistols rode up to the front gate. Both looked saddle weary; their lips were parched and their faces sunburned. Obviously the men were kin—brothers, likely. And they looked familiar to me, especially the one with a small mole on his cheek.

> "I looked over Jordan
> And what did I see?
> Coming for to carry me home,
> A band of angels coming after me,
> Coming for to carry me home."

Aunt Gran stopped singing and eyed those strangers with curiosity and caution. Then I heard her mumble something that sounded to me like *"Wolves?"* before she went out to greet the men. "Mornin'."

"Mornin', miss ma'am," one of them said, taking off his hat in a gentlemanly way. "Do you know of a place where we might rent a room for the night? Get a bite to eat?"

Porch Lies

Aunt Gran wiped her brow with her forearm, all the time studying the young men. "And by the looks of you, you need to be doc-
tored on," she said, pointing to a bloody bandage around the arm of
the man with the mole.

"We do at that," said the one doing the talking.

Aunt Gran was slow to speak again. "Well, first, 'fore I go to giving out information, tell me, who might you be?"

The injured man slid off his horse effortlessly. He touched the
handle of his six-shooter. "I'm John Howard and this is my brother,
Tom. We're businessmen from Missouri."

Then it hit me, and my heart skipped two beats—I'd seen wanted
posters for them in town! Right in front of us was none other than
the notorious duo Frank and Jesse James, the toughest outlaws ever
to rob a bank or hold up a train. Every marshal, every sheriff, every
Pinkerton detective in the country was looking for them.

Aunt Gran didn't seem to realize that the one with the mole, who
called himself John Howard, was really Jesse James and that Tom
was Frank. And there was no way for me to warn her.

"Howard?" she said, tilting her head. "Can't say I know any
Howards."

The men glanced at each other, conversing without actually
talking.

I watched as my aunt cupped her hands over her eyes to block
the sun's glare. "*Businessmen*, you say?" She chuckled softly. "Y'all
look more like po' farm boys to me, done strayed too far from home
and got yo'selves into something. Yo' people must be worried silly
'bout you. When's the last time you been to see 'bout yo' mama?"

Neither man answered.

Aunt Gran shifted her weight and leaned back on one leg. "I'm Mrs. Henrietta McClintock, but you can call me Aunt Gran."

Each nodded in a gesture of greeting. It was a decent move, I thought. Not one you would expect from criminals.

"I wouldn't mind you staying, but my well went brackish," Aunt Gran said. "There won't be any fresh water after I use what's in the rain barrel."

"Got nobody—no husband, no sons to help you here?" Jesse asked, looking around for signs of a man.

"Just me and my nephew."

I tried to pull myself up tall to appear older and stronger.

"Too bad," said Frank. "Tell you what. If you let us stay a few nights, I'll take a look at your well in the morning and see what can be done."

"I'm ever grateful." Aunt Gran's face brightened. "But guns and hats come off before entering my house. No women. No gambling. No swearing. No whiskey."

The brothers frowned.

"Oh, yes, and you must bathe 'fore you can eat at my table and sleep on my clean sheets."

"I thought you were low on water?" Frank replied.

"Brackish water aine drinkable, but you can still bathe in it."

"Oh. Well, I'll do anything you say, ma'am, just to sleep 'tween clean sheets." And Frank unbuckled his gun belt, adding, "Come on, brother."

Jesse was sullen. I could tell he wasn't accustomed to being told what to do, especially by an elderly black woman. "I can't be separated from my gun," he said firmly.

Porch Lies

"Aine nobody gon' disturb you lessen they get by me. And I reckon I can protect the likes of you two businessmen, don't you think?" Aunt Gran said with a nod and a wink.

His scowl turned into a full grin. "Aunt Gran, I have no doubt that you can handle anything comes your way." And to my surprise Jesse James took off his gun belt and handed it over.

"Come," she said, "let me doctor on that arm."

And Jesse obeyed my little five-foot-two auntie like a first grader following his teacher.

Meanwhile, Frank handed me the reins to their horses. "You got a name?" he asked.

"I'm Junior."

"How much to take care of our horses, Junior?"

"Nothing, sir!"

Looking at me from under bushy eyebrows, he added in a low voice, "You know who we are, don't you?"

"Sure," I answered quickly. "A couple of businessmen passing through."

Frank tossed me a coin and bounced up the steps, calling over his shoulder, "That's right, and don't you forget it."

After baths in hot salty water and a meal of chicken and dumplings, the James brothers slept for hours. I had plenty of time to tell Aunt Gran who they really were.

"That's Frank and Jesse James, wanted train and bank robbers," I whispered. "There's a reward on their heads. We could turn them in and use the reward money to pay off the taxes, get a new well dug, a new fence built, and still have change. I could slip out the back door—"

"Stop, stop!" Aunt Gran held up her hands. Then she sucked her teeth and gave me a disappointed look. "I would rather lose everything than betray a trust."

"But these are out*laws*, Aunt Gran. They break the *law*!"

She shushed me quiet. "You forget yo'self, Junior."

Then she calmly laced her fingers and rested her hands in her lap.

When Aunt Gran spoke again it was with patience and love. "I remember the family who broke the law and hid me and your great-uncle in a secret room of their attic when we ran away from Mas' Webb. Hunting dogs chased us through the woods. So scared. I also know what it means to be betrayed. We almost made it to freedom, but we got captured by slave hunters fifty miles from the Canadian border. A woman who'd invited us to hide in her root cellar turned us in for the money."

"But this is different. These men are robbers," I argued.

"No different to me." Aunt Gran shook her head. "I invited the Howards into my house. They say they're businessmen. And I aine never seen a wanted poster for any Howard brothers. Have you?"

"No, ma'am."

"Then that's what you say to anybody who asks. Understand?" She patted the back of my hand. "You must trust as well as obey," she said. "Watch as well as pray."

And that was the end of that.

Porch Lies

✖✖✖✖

Morning came. Jesse was the first one at the table. "Ma'am," he said, "I thank you for allowing me to sleep in a bed with clean sheets. And my arm aine nearly as sore." He rubbed it and smiled.

About that time, Frank came in from outside. "I've been down inspecting your well, Aunt Gran. Somebody real ornery threw sacks of rock salt down there."

"Just what I thought. It was the night riders," said Aunt Gran. "They salted my well to run me off my place."

Frank looked concerned. "Ah, you don't need a new well. The one you've got is spring fed, so the running water will purify itself once the salt sacks are pulled out. Dredging a well is hard work, but it's cheaper than sinking a new one."

She commenced to wringing her hands. "I aine got no extra money to dredge a well. So I guess them Knights will win."

"That's too bad," said Jesse. "You got a real nice place here. Very beautiful view of the valley."

I was surprised that a bandit paid attention to beauty.

"How'd you come by this place?" he asked.

"The land b'longed to my ol' master and missus, Charles and Sarah Webb. He died right before the beginning of the war. Then Missus Sarah's mind broke after the Yanks burned the mansion to the ground and she couldn't find her husband's fortune. When the war ended, her brother came from Connecticut and deeded the land to us ex-slaves. That's why our settlement is called Webb Hollow."

Jesse sat up. "Go back a second. What fortune? Tell us about it," he insisted.

Aunt Gran shrugged. "Anybody in these parts can tell you about the Webb fortune. Some folk believe the story; some don't. You decide for yourself. Say to protect his money from getting into Yankee hands, Charles Webb sold off paintings and jewels and turned all his cash into gold. He buried it on the plantation somewhere in December 1860. The war started in April 1861."

"Where exactly was the plantation house?" Jesse's eyes were filled with excitement.

"My husband and I built our home—this cabin—on the ruins of the big house. The very spot where we once labored as slaves."

"Did Webb leave a map?" Frank put in.

"Just listen," said Aunt Gran. "That night when ol' Master came in after burying the treasure, he went into the library and began drawing a map. But all the digging proved too much for his heart. They found him dead at his desk the next morning, the map never completed. Missus had every slave digging for that money. Then the Yanks came and burned the plantation, including the half-completed map. That's when Missus Sarah's mind went into a dark place and never came out again."

Aunt Gran had always told me that it was a made-up story. But now here she was, telling it like it was the gospel truth. And by the hungry look on those outlaws' faces, they were eating up every word.

Frank added cream to his second cup of coffee. "What do you believe, Aunt Gran?" he asked.

After a moment of thought she answered. "I believe the real fortune is the land itself. That's why I don't want to let him have it."

Jesse's eyes turned the color of a cloudy sky. "Who?"

"We're being deviled by a man named Green Farley."

The name seemed to startle Jesse, and he automatically reached for the gun he wasn't wearing. Checking the wall rack to make sure his gun was in clear sight, he broke in, "*Green Farley?* Lanky fellow? Red hair? Long nose with beady green weasel-eyes?"

"Uh-huh," said Aunt Gran. "That's Farley, all right. Do you know him?"

"Does he have a scar on his forehead that looks like a bolt of lightning?" Frank asked.

Aunt Gran nodded.

"Ha!" Frank laughed. "My brother put it there."

"If it's the same Farley who served with us during the war, he's the spawn of a rattler," Jesse said between clenched teeth. "Nobody who rode with us liked Farley. Nobody, not even snakes, who are his next of kin."

Frank picked up from there. "Hey, kid," he said to me. "Ever hear of William Clarke Quantrill?"

"Yes, sir, I heard of him. Commanded a troop of Confederate guerilla fighters—hit and run, always on the move."

"Those fighters was us," Frank said. "And Farley, too. We lost track of him, until now."

"Maybe . . ." Aunt Gran's voice trailed off.

"Maybe what? Go on. Tell us."

"Maybe you should come to a meeting with me tonight," she suggested.

I was outdone when they accepted. Could these really be the terrible James brothers? Right now, they seemed more the way Aunt

Gran had described them the day they rode up—poor farm boys who'd strayed too far from home.

✕✕✕✕

Mr. Abraham Simms chaired the meeting. As a hush fell over the room, he asked Aunt Gran to introduce her guests.

"As you know, my well was salted earlier this week. But Mr. Tom Howard," Aunt Gran said, pointing to Jesse, "and Mr. John Howard"—she pointed to Frank—"came along. These two business-men have taken the time out of their busy schedule to hear our problems."

People applauded with smiles all around.

"It seems the Howards know Green Farley, and they want to hear what he and the Knights have done."

There was a collective gasp, and people started whispering and talking all excited-like, going on about how their coming to Webb Hollow was a miracle.

And before the evening was over, the citizens had poured their hearts out to the Howards, telling them everything Farley had done to make their lives miserable.

As they listened, Jesse and Frank looked at each other in that way they had of communicating without talking.

At last, Mr. Simms went over to the brothers. "Thank you for coming, Mr. Howard and Mr. Howard," he said. "Please, enjoy your stay at Aunt Gran's. She's a marvelous cook."

"Don't we know it," said Jesse.

While others were talking to Frank and Jesse, Mr. Simms pulled

Aunt Gran to the side. "Do you know who those men are?" I over-heard him ask her.

Aunt Gran answered him the same way she had me. "They are who they say they are. The Howards."

"I see what you mean," he said, smiling.

I whispered to Willie Watkins, "Aunt Gran thinks we're deaf, dumb, and blind. Everybody knows the Howards are the James brothers."

Willie gave me a serious look and shook his head. "Boy, take a hint from an old fool. If Aunt Gran say them is General Grant and General Lee, then that's who they be till she say they ain't."

At sunrise, Frank and Jesse were up, asking for rope and shovels and buckets. "We've decided to stay and give you a hand with your well."

"Glory be," said Aunt Gran. I thought she'd be happy, but her face looked otherwise. "I don't have no money to pay you with."

"Who asked for money?" said Frank. "We're going to dredge it and try to get the salt out. Once that's done, it should cleanse itself in a day or so."

"But there is one thing we'd like in return," Jesse put in.

"Name it."

"We'd like to dig round on your place and see if we might find . . . you know, the fortune," he whispered, as though it was a big secret.

Aunt Gran shook her head. "Is that all? Well, help yo'self." She dismissed them with a wave of her dish towel.

Our guests worked all day, stopping only for lunch. Then they dug for gold.

"Don't work too late. I'm having pigs' feet for supper," said Aunt Gran as she picked an apronful of early greens.

"Pickled, I hope," said Jesse. "I love pickled pigs' feet."

At supper, Frank sucked the juice from the last bone, then polished it off with a big glass of buttermilk. "We didn't find anything today," he said, wiping his mouth with his sleeve. "I say we need a plan."

Jesse agreed, sopping his biscuit in honey. "But I feel we're close. I have a nose for gold," he said. "And my nose is twitching the way it does when gold is nearby."

"I'm really tired," said Frank. "I b'lieve I'll turn in. We'll get started early again in the morning."

The brothers went to bed, but they didn't go to sleep. When the house was quiet and the whippoorwills were calling, I heard them slip downstairs and put on their gun belts, which were hanging by the door. Easing out, Jesse said to Frank, "You better believe ol' Farley's trying to get his hands on this land for a reason, and it aine got nothing to do with a paper mill."

"Think he knows about the Webb treasure?" Frank asked.

"I'd bet a team of Missouri mules on it," Jesse said. "Let's just pay ol' Farley a visit and see to it that he takes his business elsewhere. The last thing we need is that low-life crook getting in the way of our action."

"What if he refuses?" Frank asked.

"Now, brother, you know I aine one to take no for an answer."

They laughed as they slipped away into the darkness.

I wasn't the only one who overheard their conversation. Just then Aunt Gran let go with a hearty laugh and said out loud, "Lawd! Thank you for sending us the help we need!"

✕✕✕✕

It was 'long 'bout then that I began to suspect that Aunt Gran knew more than she was letting on. Was it divine intervention, or was all this part of a scheme to get a wolf to drive out a fox? Could Aunt Gran have used the fictitious story about a lost treasure to stir up Frank and Jesse James's interest in protecting her property so they could hunt for gold? Everything was made easier when it turned out Frank and Jesse already knew and disliked Farley.

All I know is that after that night, Farley wasn't heard from again. Say he was seen slinking away from town like a whupped dog. No signs of them Knights, either.

With Farley gone it felt like a big weight was lifted off the people's heads. Their spirits were raised, and they all knew who they had to thank for it.

But Frank and Jesse never said a mumbling word. They just kept working on Aunt Gran's well. Several weeks later, the Jameses were still with us. The well had long since begun to give fresh, cool, clear, drinkable springwater. But they continued to dig for gold from sunup till sundown—with no luck. I was beginning to wonder if they were ever going to leave.

Then one day, after a big supper of fried catfish and hush puppies, Aunt Gran thanked the brothers for their generous help. Then she added tactfully, "Now, when did you say you was leaving?"

×××××

The brothers thought it best to travel at night. "Too many folks trying to be outlaws these days," said Frank. "A man can't get around safely in broad daylight anymore."

We were all standing at the door, saying our good-byes, when the brothers exchanged glances, then turned to Aunt Gran. "We have an offer for you," Jesse began.

Frank completed the idea. "We'd like to come back and search for the lost gold."

"I don't know 'bout that, Mr. Howard," said Aunt Gran reluctantly.

Huh-oh, I thought. *The wolves are not willing to go.*

"Look, we'll give you a four-dollar advance," Jesse said, offering her money. "And four dollars each time we come."

"We promise not to wear out our welcome," Frank put in, grinning widely.

Aunt Gran refused the money and backed away, shaking her head. "Can't do it!"

"Why? Not enough? What about a five-dollar digging fee?"

"No, it's not the money."

"Maybe she don't trust us," Frank said, his eyes dancing playfully. "You think we'll take all the gold for ourselves?"

Aunt Gran fanned him away like a pesky fly. "You know better."

I could see worry mounting in her eyes as Frank pushed. "I promise if we find the gold, we'll share it with you, the kid . . . the whole town."

"I can't let you dig up my yard like that."

Jesse was getting anxious. "We could just do it! You know who we are, don't you?"

Aunt Gran never raised her voice. "To me, you'll always be two Missouri farm boys who strayed too far from home."

Jesse dropped his head.

Aunt Gran flopped into her rocking chair. She appeared small and tired. "My conscience won't let me agree to it. Here's why. I told you that lost fortune story so you'd have a reason to stay on and protect my farm, my timber. I used you to get rid of Farley."

"None of the story was true?" Frank asked, looking like a disappointed child.

"Some part of it mighta been true at one time, but now it's just a tale that's been told so many times nobody knows the truth. I'd be sending you on a fool's errand if I didn't tell you any better."

As Aunt Gran talked, Jesse's eyes became narrow slits. I braced for what might happen.

Frank stood very still, like a cat in a storm. The two brothers glanced at each other, then at us. Jesse's hand slid to his gun handle. Frank stepped between Aunt Gran and me. I made my peace, 'cause I felt sure we were about to meet our Maker.

Then, all of a sudden, Jesse commenced to laughing. Frank started up, too. Before we knew it, they were bent over hee-hawing with laugh tears running down their faces.

Aunt Gran and I just watched in wonder.

At last, Jesse pulled himself together long enough to continue. "Aunt Gran, you almost got me. You just about convinced me. But I remembered something you said when you told us about Webb's fortune: *some folk believe the story; some don't. You decide for yourself.* You don't believe the story. But guess what? We do!"

Before Aunt Gran could speak another word, Jesse placed a five-dollar gold piece in her palm and closed her hand with a squeeze and a wink. "We'll be back."

Aunt Gran sighed, then chuckled in that way she had. "Fine. But you can't say I didn't tell you. Now my conscience is clear. You two gophers can dig round out there long as you please. But remember, whenever you show up, my rules are the same. Guns off at the door. No women. No gambling. No swearing. No whiskey. And you must bathe."

"You drive a hard bargain," said Frank, returning her grin and touching the brim of his hat.

"Until next time," Aunt Gran said, waving good-bye.

As she leaned back in her rocker, she said to me, "Junior, you must trust as well as obey. Watch as well as pray."

✕✕✕✕✕

It's common knowledge that Aunt Gran adopted Frank and Jesse James, although she always called them John and Tom Howard. They visited her and the citizens of Webb Hollow regularly to rest, heal, eat pickled pigs' feet, and of course, dig for treasure. And no-body bothered our little town ever again, so we prospered and grew.

The digging fees Frank and Jesse paid ensured that Aunt Gran always had her tax money. They never found their gold.

Today, the only thing left to show that there ever was a place called Webb Hollow is the Mount Nebo Cemetery and this story. Some believe it. Some don't. I'll let you decide. Before you make up your mind, let me tell you this: one of the largest stones still standing in that cemetery is an angel with outstretched wings, inscribed:

HENRIETTA MCCLINTOCK
OUR BELOVED "AUNT GRAN"

According to cemetery records, the stone was bought and paid for by Frank James.

BY THE WEIGHT
OF A FEATHER

Dedicated to Sarilda Blake
and Reverend January Kiefer,
who helped me with this story

I never knew a nicer, kinder man than Mr.
Chester Marcus, who owned the local grocery store.

Back then, neighborhood grocery stores delivered to their customers. Although Mr. Marcus had employees, it wasn't uncommon for him to make a few deliveries himself. I loved it when he came to our house, usually bringing a porch lie with our groceries.

During one visit, Mr. Marcus told us he'd recently been to a twenty-fifth wedding anniversary party. "It was lovely," he said, smiling. "What made it special was that twenty-five years ago everybody said the marriage wouldn't last a month."

Then he settled back. I got comfortable.

"This is the happy couple's story," he began. "It's one of my favorites, because it reminds me to be careful 'bout the way I judge other people, and the way I judge myself. Remember, there's good and bad in all of us. . . ."

Porch Lies

✕✕✕✕

When I was about ten or so, my mother opened a boardinghouse over on the south side near the university. One of her regulars was Clovis Reed, a used-car salesman with a less than sterling reputation. Everybody warned Mama that if Clovis got half a chance, he'd sell her a cabbage and convince her it was lettuce. The man had a gift.

Mama knew all about his questionable character but chose to ignore it. She liked Clovis, and so did I.

Even though he was a grown-up, Clovis didn't act like one, never expecting me to use correct English or stand up straight. He took me bridge-fishing over in Bristol County, taught me how to play penny poker and how to whistle through my teeth. He told the best scary stories in the world and then sat with me until I went to sleep. Clovis was the big brother I never had.

Then Clovis went and asked Mae June Lawson to marry him. It didn't surprise anybody that he'd asked such a sophisticated, pretty girl. After all, most of the eligible young men in town had done the same. Mae June'd turned them all down.

Oh, but didn't the tongues start to wagging when she accepted Clovis's proposal! The town gossips had a big bone to chew on for days.

It's fair to say that at first glance, the two of them didn't seem suited for each other. In fact, they were the least likely people anybody would have put together. Like I said, Mae June was a pretty girl, smart, popular, and from a good home. She'd learned typing at a trade school in the big city of Chicago. Learned how to dress smartly, too. She came back to Briarsville on account of her sick mother and got a job as the secretary for the only black lawyer in town.

As for Clovis, he went in the front door and out the back of several schools, and I don't think he'd traveled past middle Tennessee. His mama'd died giving birth to him, and the boy carried the guilt of it. His father didn't make it any better, either. "You're just like my daddy and me, so you're bound to be a loser!" James Reed prophesied.

Then one day, Reed walked off and left Clovis on his own at the age of twelve. From that day forward, the boy seemed to do everything he could to fulfill the awful inheritance his father had left him.

Clovis lived with one family after another until he finally ended up in an orphanage. "You'll come to no good," said the principal of his school, just before expelling the sixteen-year-old.

Then Clovis started selling things—anything to make a dime. See, selling came natural to him. Finally, he got a job selling used cars at Top of the Hill Used Auto Park, owned by Clyde Givens.

Givens taught Clovis every trick of the used-car trade, and in a way he became the parent Clovis never had. Givens wasn't much of a role model. He lived it up and died young, leaving his business—what remained of it—to Clovis.

For the young man, dealing in used cars turned out to be a blessing and a curse. At first, Clovis did a'right for himself. But then came a long string of bad incidents that didn't help his reputation.

"You're a low-down, rotten cheat," yelled an ex-girlfriend.

"You're a no-good swindler," said a client.

"You're a thief . . . a liar . . ."

It went on and on.

Adding to this, Clovis was now turning thirty years old, and had already lived the life of a forty-five-year-old, what with wild parties, gambling, and the like. Needless to say, not too many folks thought he was good husband material for any woman, least of all the town's sweetheart.

Even so, Mae June was his number one supporter. "Clovis always lifts my spirits. He makes me laugh," she told Reverend Beasley, who tried to convince her to turn down Clovis's proposal.

Based on the conversations I overheard on the front porch, most of the townsfolk thought Mae June had lost a few marbles while she was off in the big city.

"Why would a pretty little thing like that want to marry a used-car salesman who's known for slicking people?" asked Mis Kingsbury, who had never been married.

"No telling what he's promised her," said Mrs. Granger, who had been three times divorced.

"That marriage aine gon' last a month," speculated Mrs. Townsend, sucking in air and blowing it out forcefully. She failed to mention that her own marriage hadn't lasted much longer.

But Mama didn't agree with the naysayers. "I think it's just what Clovis needs—a good woman to share his life with. She'll press out all the wrinkles."

So the wedding invitations were sent. The cake ordered. The rehearsal held. Everything was ready.

On the night before the big wedding, too excited to sleep, I went downstairs to get a drink of water. To my surprise, I saw Clovis creeping down the steps carrying a suitcase.

"Where you goin', Clov?" I said from the darkness.

"Wha—Who . . . Chester?" he stammered.

I switched on the light.

He hurriedly switched it off, then flopped onto the couch like a heavy sack of potatoes. "I can't marry that girl," he said, woefully sad.

"You're running off?" I'd never felt so disappointed in my life. "Clovis, why?"

"I don't want to destroy Mae June's life, and I'm going 'fore it's too late. She'll be better off without a wreck like me hanging around her neck," he whispered, more to himself than to me. "By leaving, I'll be doing what everybody expects me to do anyway."

"Don't go, Clovis," I begged. "You aine *that* bad."

"Chester," he said, tilting his head to the side, "you don't have any idea. If I found myself standing before judgment this very night, I would be in serious trouble." He headed for the door.

"Wait," I said, tugging at his arm. "I bet I could get four . . . three . . . a couple of people to say you're as decent as a preacher . . . a judge . . . a nice person, maybe."

That line of reasoning seemed a bit weak, so I changed my approach. "Don't go tonight," I began again. "Sleep on it, and if you wake up in the morning and you still want to slink away like a sniveling coward, then you'll have time to crawl out the back way. Please?"

Clovis thought for a minute, then reluctantly agreed. He went back upstairs to his bedroom, and I followed and sat on the floor outside his door the rest of the night, just to make sure he didn't change his mind.

At dawn I heard him stirring. I knocked softly.

"What! Who is it?" he called, sounding somewhat shaken.

"It's me, Chester."

"Oh, thank goodness. Come on in."

Clovis was sitting on the side of the bed. His hands covered his face and he needed a shave. "What's today?" he asked.

"Your wedding day?" I posed it as a question.

Clovis hopped out of bed, ran to the window, and yelled out, "Yes! It is! My wedding day. I'm turning over a new leaf, 'cause look, Chester! *The grass is green.*"

What? What did that mean? Had Clovis gone mad?

One look at his face and I realized he was filled with true joy.

"I guess you came to your senses," I said.

"You might say that," he said, smiling.

"What happened?" I asked.

Then Clovis Reed told me the astonishing story of what had occurred during the night.

As soon as Clovis had closed his door, he'd fallen across his bed. Lying on his back looking up at the blank ceiling, he tried to figure out what to do. Should he or shouldn't he marry Mae June? He'd never had this kind of trouble before, and his mind was in total confusion.

From somewhere in the distance Clovis heard a clock strike

twelve times. Before the sound of the twelfth chime faded, his room was bathed in a ghostly blue light.

The young man sat up, startled, but not frightened. (He'd never been scared since as a young boy he'd taken on the biggest kid in school and won.) "Can you still sell the president a pair of red pajamas?" Mrs. Helene Bumpers, his sixth-grade teacher, asked, moving out of the swirling blue light.

"Clovis Reed, is that you, you jive turkey?" added Defoe Reynolds, stepping out of the blue light behind Mrs. Bumpers. "You still selling bum cars? That one you sold me lasted 'bout three days and died. If only I'd read the small print on the contract. You just wait. It's payback time."

Clovis rose from bed as Mrs. Bumpers and Defoe Reynolds vanished. They were dead . . . so how did they get in his bedroom? Something was way wrong. Clovis decided that he'd better put on his shoes just in case he needed to escape.

Suddenly there was a knock at his door.

"Who is it?"

"Alonzo Wiggins, Esquire," a man called back, sliding his card underneath the door. "I hope I'm not late for the proceedings."

Clovis picked up the card and read it. "An attorney-at-law? I don't need no blasted lawyer!"

"Well, yes, Mr. Reed. It seems you do."

Clovis opened the door a crack. Alonzo Wiggins pushed it all the way open, then strode past him, showing no concern for the strange blue light that bathed the entire room.

Standing side by side, the two men were opposite extremes of height and weight—Clovis, short, stocky, and built like an Olympic champion; Alonzo Wiggins, tall and thin. His large, protruding eyes set far apart in a pie-shaped face gave him a froglike appearance. Both men shared the same prominent African nose and coffee-colored skin. Clovis couldn't help but think that he'd never have tagged Wiggins for a lawyer. He was more the undertaker type. Yes, thought Clovis, Mr. Wiggins reminded him of an undertaker he'd played poker with in Chicago a while back. But his name wasn't Wiggins. *Or was it?*

"Okay, okay," said Clovis. "What's this? Some joke the guys are playing on me?"

"I assure you this is no joking matter," said Mr. Wiggins. "You need to come with me, Mr. Reed."

"Naw, naw, naw. You got to tell me where we going first," Clovis said, pulling back.

Mr. Wiggins pointed to the swirling vortex in the blue light. "There."

Clovis shook his head. "I'm silly at times, but I aine dumb. I'm not going into . . . into whatever that thing is. No, sir." He was emphatic.

But as Clovis stood protesting, the bedroom in which he and Mr. Wiggins were standing was transforming itself into a courtroom, complete with bailiff, judge's bench, witness box, table, and chairs.

Now Clovis was truly scared. "I didn't move my legs. How did I get here? And wh-wh-who's on trial?"

Mr. Wiggins took a stack of papers from his briefcase.

"You are," he answered. "And I've been appointed your lawyer."

"Me? What have I been charged with? What did I do?"

Mr. Wiggins shook his head and sighed. "It seems you've done plenty. You've been charged with all manner of mischief—from wasting your own life to making life miserable for others. But don't worry, I've prepared a good defense."

Clovis was about to argue, but Mr. Wiggins raised a finger to silence him.

"All rise," said the bailiff, "for Judge William Montgomery Jones, also known as the Honorable Will Hang You Jones."

The judge entered, looking as stern as his name implied. Clovis's wobbly legs threatened to give way when he realized that the judge reminded him of his high school principal from years back. But his name wasn't Jones. *Or was it?*

The bailiff placed brass scales and a basket of feathers beside the judge. All the time, Clovis couldn't keep his eyes off the bailiff, who could have been Henry Washington's twin. Henry was a quarterback in high school who got cut from the team after breaking curfew with Clovis. But this wasn't Henry. *Or was it?*

"What in the ham fat is going on?" Clovis blurted out.

Mr. Wiggins shushed Clovis.

The judge began. "We are here today to weigh the life of one Clovis Ambrose Reed, a sometime salesman by profession, a slickster by design."

"Salesman," shouted the court stenographer. "Is that what they call crooks these days?"

Taking a closer look, Clovis saw that the woman speaking resembled Mae June's mother, Miz Theola. But it wasn't really her. *Or was it?*

Clovis was so confused, he pinched Mr. Wiggins and then himself. When Mr. Wiggins cried out in pain, Clovis figured they were both awake.

The judge knocked three times with his gavel. "No outbursts

will be tolerated during these proceedings. I want order in this court," he demanded in a stern voice. "Let's get on with it!"

"Your Honor," began Mr. Wiggins. "I would like to move that the court dismiss this case based on the no-fault clause."

"What is your evidence?" the judge asked.

"I have a witness who would like to address the court," said Mr. Wiggins.

"Mr. James Thomas Reed," announced the bailiff.

The doors swung open and there he stood.

"Daddy?" cried Clovis, leaping to his feet. "Is that you, for real?" Clovis hadn't seen his father in years. How short he seemed compared to what Clovis remembered! All the swagger was gone out of his step. He was older, he had less hair, and his back was bent as though, like Atlas, he was postured to carry the world on his shoulders.

James Reed came to the witness stand, and with some difficulty, he swore to tell the truth.

A wave of anger overwhelmed Clovis and he burst into sputtering laughter. "Truth! What does *he* know about truth?"

The judge shot Clovis a nasty look, and Clovis sat down without uttering another word.

"Son, I know how you must feel," James Reed began gently, looking at Clovis. His eyes were rimmed in red. Turning to the court, he confessed what a poor father he had been. "I deserted my boy when he needed me the most. But I've come here today to say: whatever Clovis has done wrong in his life is my fault. Blame me. Punish me. Please show mercy and dismiss the case, sir."

The judge listened closely. When Mr. Reed was done, the judge pulled himself tall in his chair and spoke forcefully, with deep conviction. "James Reed, truly, truly, you were a miserable father! But it is not a parent's duty to assume the guilt of his or her child." The judge rapped his gavel. "Request denied!"

Clovis watched his father leave the courtroom without saying a word.

"Sorry the motion didn't pass," said Mr. Wiggins. "It was a long shot, but worth trying. I hope this helps your father rest in peace."

"Daddy is dead?" Clovis was shocked. "How long?"

"Seven years," said Mr. Wiggins.

"Then how could he be here with me . . . ?" Clovis pounded his fist on the table. "This is crazy!"

"I apologize for my client," Mr. Wiggins said to the judge. "He's under the misconception that this is a regular court, sir. He doesn't seem to understand the gravity of his situation. May we have a short recess, so I may enlighten him?"

"Ten minutes, no more." The honorable Will Hang You Jones slammed the gavel down with a force that shook the room.

✖✖✖✖

Mr. Wiggins didn't waste any time impressing upon Clovis the importance of the proceedings. "Your life is being judged like an open book. The good and bad that you've done will be examined and weighed. For each good deed, a feather is placed on the right side of the scale. For each misdeed, one will be placed on the left. In the end, your own deeds will judge you. If need be, Judge Jones will then sentence you accordingly."

Porch Lies

When Clovis and his lawyer returned to the courtroom, Clovis was subdued. Actually, he was terrified.

"Next witness is Mrs. Alva Evans," said the bailiff.

Mrs. Evans, one of Clovis's very first customers, hobbled forward. She was very old and hardly able to walk. Clovis remembered that she was a sweet lady with kind eyes and a gentle manner.

"I do," she swore, stating that her testimony would be true.

Mrs. Evans gave the defendant a look of total disappointment. "Clovis, Clovis, Clovis. Remember when you were thirteen and you sold me a tea set—a tray and a teapot with four cups and saucers—and you told me it was real china?" She pointed a shaking finger. "Yes, yes, you did. And so I used money from my food budget to buy the set. It took Portia Newtower, of all people, to tell me it was nothing but fake. To add insult to misery, Portia announced it in front of all our quilting bee members. 'Alma,' she says, 'you've been taken for a ride. This tea set is not worth fifteen cents.' "

"Any rebuttal?" the judge asked Mr. Wiggins.

"No, Your Honor."

"I was just a kid!" Clovis shouted.

The judge placed a feather on the left side of the scale. It tilted that way. "You were old enough to know right from wrong," he said, adding crossly, "One more outburst and you'll be sorry."

Clovis groaned and dabbed at his head with a tissue. He turned to Mr. Wiggins. "How come you didn't defend me? Mrs. Evans paid two-ninety-nine for that little tea set. She should have known it wasn't real china. It's not my fault she wasn't an informed buyer."

"Mrs. Evans is not the one on trial here," said Mr. Wiggins. "Just be patient."

"Mr. Clive Green," the bailiff called.

Mr. Green walked to the witness stand and was sworn in. For a while the Greens had been Clovis's neighbors.

"When we moved to Briarsville," began Mr. Green after being sworn in, "my son was small and wore glasses, and the bigger kids called him names and picked fights. He didn't want to go to school, and he wasn't learning while he was there. Then Clovis started walking Tommy to and from school every day. Clovis defended our boy, and even got in trouble for standing up to bigger boys who tried to take Tommy's lunch money. Today, our son is a doctor, but I wonder what would have happened if Clovis had not befriended him."

Clovis had almost forgotten little Thomas Green. "So he's a doctor now? That's good." Clovis gave Mr. Green a thumbs-up. "I always knew Tommy was going to do well."

Judge Will Hang You Jones placed a feather on the right side of the scale and it came into balance.

Clovis smiled.

For an hour or more, witnesses gave testimony about Clovis Reed—some good, some bad. The scales dipped accordingly—to the right, then back to the left, and back again to the right. Teachers, neighbors, team members, employers, classmates, on and on the testimony mounted.

Defoe Reynolds finished, telling the story of how Clovis sold him a clunker from Top of the Hill Used Auto Park, knowing that it wasn't any good. "It was an *r*, not a *car*, because the *c* and *a* fell off of it," Defoe complained.

The judge placed a feather on the left side and tipped the scales.

"Told you I'd get you back." Defoe sneered at Clovis.

When the judge asked if Mr. Wiggins wanted to question the witness, he passed. Clovis tried to stay calm, but what kind of lawyer didn't cross-examine witnesses?

Mrs. Estella Granberry was called. As she approached the witness stand, Clovis couldn't be quiet any longer. "I know she's gon' talk about that car battery thing," he said to Mr. Wiggins.

After being sworn in, Mrs. Granberry began giving testimony in her best storytelling voice. "Imagine this. It was the coldest night on record in the city. Car batteries were failing all over the neighborhood, but the battery in *my* Buick turned the motor over without a problem."

"Get to the point," ordered the judge.

Mrs. Granberry cooled herself with a church fan. "Well, to make a long story short," she said, rolling her eyes at the judge, "Clovis Reed stole the battery out of my car. Mind you, I have asthma *and* high blood pressure. I tremble to think of what might have happened if I'd had an attack and needed to get to the hospital. The whole thing was so upsetting, I nearly had a stroke."

Clovis jumped out of his seat again. "I didn't *steal* your battery. I borrowed it, and you know why."

Judge Will Hang You Jones beat his gavel so hard, the sound reverberated off the walls and made the room shake twice as much as before.

"You took it without permission, you rascal," Mrs. Granberry snapped, refusing to back down. "You left me without a way to get to the hospital if I needed to. I could have died."

Now the judge was on his feet. "The witness and the defendant will not address each other again. In fact, there will not be another word spoken in this courtroom until I say so," he shouted. And the room rocked and swayed on its foundation. Plaster cracked and fell in chunks.

Then the room was silent.

"Clovis Reed," the judge asked, "did you take Mrs. Granberry's car battery without asking?"

"Yes, but—"

"No ifs, ands, or buts. Did you or did you not take her car battery without permission?"

"I took it," Clovis muttered.

The judge put another feather on the left side of the scale.

It took a lot of restraint for Clovis to be still. It wasn't until the bailiff called Lawrence Logan to testify that he settled down a bit. He knew Lawrence would bring out his side of the story.

Lawrence looked impressive, dressed in his Sunday best. He spoke softly but confidently. "One cold January night my wife woke up suffering terrible chest pains. Clovis and I aine never really been that close, but on that night, I asked if he'd drive us to the hospital. My battery was dead. His battery was dead. So he knocked on Mrs. Granberry's door, but she didn't—or wouldn't—answer. So he borrowed her battery and left a note explaining what he was doing, and why. If Clovis hadn't gotten my wife to the ER when he did, she would have died."

"And I did thirty days in the county workhouse to pay for whatever wrong I did. But if I had it to do over again, I would," Clovis added.

The judge gave him a look that said shut up. But Clovis also thought he caught a glimpse of something else in the judge's eyes— understanding.

Porch Lies

The judge removed the feather he'd just placed on the left side and moved it over to the right. The scales were perfectly balanced again. "He might hang me, but I think this judge is fair," Clovis whispered to Mr. Wiggins.

All told, twelve people had come forward to speak a word about Clovis Reed.

"How am I doing?" Clovis asked Mr. Wiggins.

"Perfect tie," he answered. "There will have to be a tiebreaker."

"Who will that be?" Clovis asked. "Who is the one person who holds my life in the balance?"

Before the lawyer could answer, the judge banged his gavel again, harder still.

"According to ancient rules, the defense attorney gets to call one witness as the tiebreaker," said the judge. "Who do you call?"

"The defense calls Barbara Davis," said Mr. Wiggins.

"Barbara Davis," said the bailiff.

"Barbara Davis?" Clovis said through clenched teeth. "Who in the world is she?"

As Miss Davis walked to the witness stand, Clovis couldn't help but notice how much she resembled Mae June. She was small framed, with soft, rounded features. "I never knew your name until today," she said. "I always thought you were an angel, Clovis."

The somber bailiff covered his mouth to conceal a smile. Even Will Hang You faked a coughing spell and turned his head to sneak a quick chuckle. Nobody had ever put *angel* and *Clovis* in the same sentence. The idea was hilarious, but Barbara Davis was not trying to be funny.

She continued. "You don't remember me, I know. We only met once at a bus stop several years ago. The Madison bus?"

Clovis nodded. He was beginning to remember—how fresh and dainty the young woman had appeared that morning! But he didn't remember Barbara looking so much like Mae June then. She had looked sad and depressed. In fact, Clovis had decided not to flirt with her, even though she was very pretty.

"I was deeply troubled back then," the young woman recalled. "I wanted to give up. Nothing had meaning for me anymore. I was ready to die, wanted to die. But you saved my life."

"And how did he do that?" the judge asked.

The Mae June look-alike faced Clovis with loving eyes. "For some unknown reason, you—Clovis—turned to me and said, 'Look, it's spring. The grass is coming up and it's green.' "

"What?" said the judge. "How did that save your life? Be careful, young lady, I don't allow nonsense in my court."

Barbara smiled and continued calmly. "No nonsense, Your Honor. Clovis's words gave me hope and a reason to go on. He reminded me that spring is about new life, new beginnings."

Then she turned back to Clovis and continued. It was as though Mae June and not Barbara was speaking to him. "And when you talked about the grass, I remembered that I could count on certain truths: the blue sky, the bright sun, and the green grass of spring. I went home determined to give life a fresh, new start. And I never got to say thank you until now."

Clovis recalled the incident the way one recalls a dream and wonders whether it really happened. "Maybe I'm not as bad as I thought," he told Mr. Wiggins.

"Why should I give credit to Clovis for a good deed that he didn't even *know* he was doing?" demanded Will Hang You.

Mr. Wiggins sprang to his feet. "Your Honor, Clovis Reed deserves credit for this kindness. Do we think the bee is unworthy of praise because it is unaware it is pollinating the flowers? I rest my case."

Mr. Wiggins took a seat. Clovis smiled admiringly. "Mighty fine lawyering," he whispered.

It was all in the hands of the judge now. The Honorable Will Hang You Jones picked up a feather and placed it on the good side. The scale tipped to the right. "Saved by the weight of a single feather," he said.

"What happens now?" Clovis asked Mr. Wiggins.

But already the blue swirling light had returned and overtaken the courtroom.

"You aren't as bad as some people say you are," said Mr. Wiggins as he faded into the haze. "But you aren't as good as you can be, either. Remember your own words: *It's spring. The grass is coming up and it's green.* Let today be the spring of your life."

"What a strange dream," I said.

Clovis was jumping around like a mad squirrel. "I'm not messing this up," he shouted. "Look happy, Chester! Today is my wedding day."

Then Clovis fell back on his pillow. "What a dream! What a dream!" He was laughing and shouting and I was laughing, too. But we both stopped when a single white feather fluttered down from overhead.

A GRAVE SITUATION

Dedicated to the memory
of Uncle B. J. Crossley,
who inspired this story

Whenever Dr. Beatrice Perriman visited
*Meharry Medical College in Nashville—which was two or three times
a year—she spent an afternoon with my grandmother, from whom she
had rented a room during her medical school years. Dr. Perriman was
the first black female doctor any of us had ever known. She was an
extraordinary cardiologist and a mesmerizing storyteller. Listening to
Dr. Perriman telling a porch lie made her seem more approachable.*

*A favorite story of mine that she told was about a man named
Lincoln James Murphy and his employer, Mis Crickett Thompson. Dr.
Perriman's mother was convinced that "Link" Murphy was a scoundrel
and a ne'er-do-well, but Dr. Perriman wasn't so sure. Here's the story
she told on our front porch in the cool of a summer evening.*

Mis Crickett Thompson was the richest somebody in Lynn Cove, Tennessee. She drove a big fancy car when most folks had to walk. She loved pretty clothes and fine jewelry—not dime-store costume jewelry, but real diamonds, pearls, rubies, and sapphires. Mama said Mis Crickett's people, the Thompsons, were old money. Her ancestors had come from England back before the United States was even a country. They were rich over there and got even richer over here. Generations later, Mis Crickett had inherited it all. Word tell she had enough money to start her own country.

Mama and both of her sisters, Gladys and Mildred, had worked for the Thompsons at one time or another—cooking, cleaning, and ironing. When I was about ten years old, Mis Crickett asked Mama if I could work for her—watering plants, sewing on a button or hemming a dress, running to the post office for stamps, and other such and such. That was the same year Lincoln James Murphy came back to Lynn Cove. He'd been away over fifteen years.

Everybody had an opinion about Lincoln Murphy, and those opinions ran from one extreme to the other. Some folks loved him. Say he was funny and good-natured. Other folks hated him. Say he was a no-good hustler.

My mama was among those who were convinced that Link was in league with the Devil himself. "Been knowing him all his sorry life," Mama said, grunting her disapproval. "Link is part snake and part weasel. Don't let that smile fool you."

Part snake, part weasel. That would make him a sneasel, I thought. The idea made me laugh. I guess I was the only person in town who didn't have an opinion one way or the other about Link Murphy.

Porch Lies

I'll never forget meeting him the day he came looking for a job with Mis Crickett Thompson.

It was 1937—the height of the Depression. Every other employer had laid people off, but Mis Crickett was hiring. She'd hired me, and then she advertised that she needed a driver to take her to Nashville once a month. She needed to go there to see a doctor 'bout some ailment she had. People didn't care why; they would have driven her to Plum-Ne'ly to buy toothpicks, because they needed the work.

Anyway, folks from miles around applied for the job, including Link Murphy. "Hear tell you need a driver," he said as he sauntered up her front walk one Friday morning. His voice was as smooth as silk, and all the time he was eyeing her green and yellow 1937 Buick. "No need to look any further. I'm yo' man."

I stood by watching as Mis Crickett raised an eyebrow suspiciously. "Mr. Murphy, what makes you think I'd trust you to drive me around the corner? Talk says you're likely to strangle me and steal my car soon as we reach the city limits."

Link dropped his head as though he'd been mortally wounded. Then he sucked in air and pulled himself tall. "You're right. You're so right, Mis Crickett." He tilted his head to the side and gave her a devilish smile. "Yes, ma'am. Can't be too careful nowadays. In fact, I was thinking on my way over here, how do I know Mis Crickett will pay me after driving her all the way to Nashville and back?"

"What?" Mis Crickett was shocked. "Are you questioning my honesty?"

Link went to twirling his hat in his hands. "No, ma'am. I was just wondering, same as you was wondering—"

Mis Crickett cut in. "But you don't even know me!"

Link didn't say another word. Didn't have to, 'cause the silence was mighty loud.

Meanwhile, I'm thinking Link's got to be addled, talking to Mis Crickett like that on a job interview.

But slowly, Mis Crickett nodded an understanding. Then she opened the screen door and let Link in.

Uh-oh, I thought. *She's let the sneasel in the henhouse.* I giggled. Link winked at me. I didn't know what to do, so I blushed.

"Come in and have a cup of tea and tell me about yourself." Mis Crickett led Link to the kitchen, where I put on a pot of water. And they spent a good while talking, those two, about everything from wild herbs to President Roosevelt.

That evening Mama had to sit down when I told her Mis Crickett had hired Link Murphy to drive her to Nashville.

"That woman is asking for trouble," she said. "You keep your eyes open, Bea. If that rascal docs anything suspicious, you bring it to me immediately."

I didn't like the idea of being a spy, but Mama insisted.

A day or two later, I had plenty to report. According to Mis Crickett, the trip to Nashville had gone well. "I don't understand why people say Link is such a terrible fellow," she said. "He's a real gentleman. Arrived on time, drove the speed limit, and never once caused me a moment of concern."

After that trip, Mis Crickett gave Link a permanent job as her chauffeur. Whenever and wherever Mis Crickett wanted to go, Link was there to take her.

Well, it wasn't long 'fore the tongues started wagging, especially after Link convinced Mis Crickett to let him keep her Buick round the clock. "I want to make sure your car is clean and polished, and have it standing ready at all times," he told Mis Crickett. And she agreed.

"See, I told you!" Mama gasped when she heard Link had started a jitney service using Mis Crickett's car. "Lawd, Lawd, that rascal done gone and turned Mis Crickett's car into a cab!"

For a dime or two, Link took people shopping at times he knew Mis Crickett wouldn't be needing her car. He drove folk to work, to church, to the doctor's office in high style. Sightings of Mis Crickett's Buick were reported in places as far away as Lebanon and Smyrna.

Word soon got to Mis Crickett, who sent me to find Link. "She's real upset," I told him. "Why didn't you ask about starting a jitney service instead of just doing it on your own?"

"Sometimes," he said, "it's easier to ask for forgiveness than to ask for permission."

Link showed up with a briefcase in his hand like he was a first-class businessman. "Well," Mis Crickett began angrily. "I hear you've gone into business using my car."

Link flashed a smile as wide as a prairie mile and popped open the briefcase. "Sorry you found out 'bout the jitney service before I had a chance to tell you myself. Truth is, Mis Crickett, I did it all on my time. Besides, I wanted to make sure it was a successful venture before I 'proached you 'bout being a full partner. Here's a breakdown of what I've made so far, what it costs, and the number of regular customers I've signed up. I'm figuring a sixty-forty split between us—what with it being yo' car and all. . . . Course I do all the work. . . ."

"The audacity!" Mis Crickett said, shaking her head in disbelief.

"Well, okay. I'll go seventy-five/twenty-five if you insist," Link said.

I held my breath, waiting for what would come next. It couldn't be anything good, I thought.

Silence. Mis Crickett looked at Link for a long, long while. Then slowly a smile broke her face like a shattering window, followed by a robust, hip-slapping laugh. "Link, you are a fox!" She looked at the papers. "Okay, you've got a deal," she said, walking away. "Sixty-five/thirty-five, and you keep all your tips. . . . I must insist. And remember, this arrangement lasts just so long as your sideline doesn't interfere with anything I've got planned and my car is kept in tip-top shape."

When I filled Mama in on all this, she was too disgusted to speak.

But in spite of all the criticism, Link's jitney service thrived. Faithfully, he brought Mis Crickett her sixty-five-percent share of the pennies, nickels, and dimes he earned in his spare time taking people to the doctor's office, the post office, the grocery store, the bus station, wherever they needed to go. I didn't know it at the time, but Mis Crickett was putting away her share of the jitney money in a bank account for my education.

Throughout that long summer, I watched an uncommon friendship develop before my eyes. When Link drove Mis Crickett, it was a spectacle. "There goes that crazy lady and Link Murphy," people would say as the two of them went rolling down Main Street, both wearing sunglasses. It was shocking at first, seeing little Mis Crickett riding up front with just the top of her head showing over the dashboard. Not even Mama had the nerve to tell her that a white lady wasn't supposed to ride up front with her black chauffeur.

Porch Lies

Police Chief Joe Sullivan thought he could. "It doesn't look right," he said to her. By the time Mis Crickett got finished quoting the Bill of Rights to him, Chief Sullivan didn't care if she rode with the president of the NAACP.

Many an evening Link and Mis Crickett sat on the front porch together, arguing politics, telling stories, and playing penny poker or checkers until the wee hours of the morning. Sometimes she read James Whitcomb Riley poetry and he'd come back with a Paul Laurence Dunbar poem. "In the Morning" was my favorite.

When Mis Crickett read stories from the literary magazine, Link nodded off in the wicker rocker and I had to wake him up. Or they took long walks in her garden at twilight. Mis Crickett was always in a good mood when Link was around.

If Link had been a white man, instead of a lean and lanky black man with a devil-may-care smile, or if Mis Crickett had been a black woman, most observers would have thought they were mother and son, or a beloved aunt and nephew. When I reported all this to Mama, she scoffed. "He's up to something. Keep yo' eyes open, Bea."

I hoped Mama was wrong.

✕✕✕✕✕

As summer faded into fall and then winter, we moved from the front porch to the parlor. There we sat by the fireplace and Mis Crickett read stories about far away and long ago. And before we knew it, the roses were blooming again.

One night I remember Mis Crickett was reading a story about

Atlas holding up the world when she stopped in the middle of a sentence. She just sat there zombie-like, her mouth open and her eyes fixed in a frozen stare. It was plenty scary. I was glad Link was there. He motioned for me to stay still and wait.

In a minute or so, as if somebody flipped a switch, Mis Crickett blinked and began reading as though nothing had happened.

"I've seen her do like that before," Link explained to me later, rather matter-of-factly. "She shorts out for a spell, like a lamp with bad wiring. Then in a snap, she's back on again."

About a week later, when Link and I arrived for one of our reading sessions, Mis Crickett's doctor and lawyer were sitting with her at the dining room table. The door was slightly cracked as if on purpose. Link and I couldn't help seeing and hearing everything from the kitchen.

Mis Crickett was signing a few papers. "It's getting progressively worse, Dr. Tate," she said. "Remember, I don't want to be embalmed or buried 'fore a week is out and until I've been pronounced dead by you and another doctor. Is that clear?"

How could he forget? She'd said it often enough. I'd heard it many times since I'd started working for her.

Then, turning to her lawyer, Goodall Harken, she continued, "Goodie"—that's what she called him—"you also remember, I want to be laid out in my good jewelry. No cheap stuff."

Goodie Harken sounded disgusted. "Now, why do you keep insisting on that? Your jewelry is worth a lot of money."

"I'd feel naked without something around my neck, rings, and a bracelet or two. Oh, and don't worry, Goodie," she added with a chuckle. "There'll be enough left over for you to sell."

"Just as you say." Mr. Harken nodded. More papers were signed.

"I'm with Mr. Harken. Hard to imagine all that pretty jewelry going in the ground," Link said to me later.

"But I can't imagine Mis Crickett without her jewelry on. She's always wearing her beads and baubles," I said.

"Them aine beads and baubles, Bea." His eyes sparkled like lights on a Christmas tree. "They're the real thing. No classy, rich lady like Mis Crickett would wear dime-store imitations."

Not long after, I caught Link up in Mis Crickett's room rambling in her jewelry box. When I questioned him about it, he flashed one of his innocent smiles. "Women aine the onlyest ones who love nice things," he said. "I aine likely to wear none of it, but I got to admit, I enjoy touching it. These here jewels is mighty pretty. Almost as pretty as you."

He knew how to make me blush. I never told Mama about that incident. After all, what was there to tell? The jewels weren't locked up. And maybe Link was just looking. Secretly, I had tried on a few pieces of Mis Crickett's jewelry myself, just to see how diamonds felt on my skin.

✕✕✕✕

One sunny morning, the first week in June, Mr. Harken came over on business and found Mis Crickett lying in her bed, completely still. It appeared she'd passed in her sleep.

No amount of badgering and bribing by Mr. Harken could get Dr. Tate to pronounce Mis Crickett dead without another doctor concurring. But Goodie Harken found a legal loophole in Mis

Crickett's papers and found two *other* doctors to sign the death certificate over Dr. Tate's protests. One had a reputation for drinking, and the other was a veterinarian. Then Goodie shamelessly began making funeral arrangements without waiting the full week. We were horrified.

"It's too soon!" I said to Link, feeling angry and confused. "Mis Crickett made them promise not to bury her inside a week and Mr. Harken knows it."

I listened from the kitchen as Link tried to speak with him, but Goodie Harken wouldn't listen. "Mis Crickett is dead. I'm in charge now," he said. "Her wake is tonight and her burial is tomorrow, and that's that."

"But, sir, you've heard her say many times she didn't want to be put away inside a week and she wanted to be laid out in her finest jewelry," Link argued. "Have you no shame?"

"How dare you speak to me that way! Who do you think you are, questioning my authority?" Goodie Harken was plenty mad. "I've put up with Mis Crickett and her silly ways for too long. Now it's my time, and I plan to enjoy every cent I'm due, starting tomorrow. She won't be any deader next week than she is now!" Then he ordered Link to leave.

Well, Link left, all right. In fact, he disappeared that very night— in Mis Crickett's Buick. Mr. Harken would have filed charges against Link for stealing, but Mis Crickett had left the car to him in her will.

None of the people Mis Crickett had depended on was doing what she asked. I was surprised Goodie granted Mis Crickett's request to be buried in her fine jewelry. Even though the diamond earrings, pearls, and gold rings she had on could have paid off

Porch Lies

Mama's mortgage, the pieces weren't her favorites, and certainly they weren't the most expensive. Goodie had held those back for himself, thinking nobody would notice. But I knew. Not only was he a liar, he was a thief.

I'd never really liked Goodie Harken, but Link Murphy was another matter. I whispered to Mama, "How could Link just leave without paying his proper respects?"

Of course, Mama and those who didn't trust Link had plenty to say. "What more can you expect from a scoundrel like him? So ungrateful," she muttered.

It really bothered me that Mama was right and that I had been such a poor judge of character. But to everybody's surprise, come morning, Link was back—just in time for the funeral. The Buick was spit polished and clean as a cat, and so was he, wearing a black suit and tie.

Link served as one of the pallbearers, and Luvella Washington sang "Amazing Grace." Then they closed Mis Crickett up, took her to the cemetery out back of the Episcopalian church, and lowered her into the ground with her jewels on. The bells tolled as Hack Long, the gravedigger, covered Mis Crickett with dirt—shovelful after shovelful after shovelful.

Hack told Mama later, "I finished my job and left. But I couldn't make Link come with me."

What nobody knew was that I hid behind a tree and watched everything that happened next.

As soon as Hack was gone, Link got a shovel and pick from the trunk of his car. I watched him dig and dig and not stop digging until he reached the coffin.

He didn't hear me slip up behind him. My heart sank when he

forced open the lid with a thud. There lay Mis Crickett in her diamond earrings, pearls, and gold rings.

"I—I didn't want to do this," I heard him say to her. "I tried to leave. In fact, I could have been long gone. But I had to come back. . . ."

Just then, Mis Crickett's eyes popped wide open!

She let out a scream that shook the very ground I stood on. Link leaped to his feet and commenced to screaming, too. I started screaming.

"You're alive!" Link shouted at Mis Crickett. "You're alive!" He turned and shouted at me, "And you're here!"

Quickly getting ahold of himself, Link began exclaiming and proclaiming, "I knew it. I knew it. I knew you was alive, Mis Crickett. I knew it."

"Oh, Link, you saved me!" Mis Crickett cried. "How will I ever be able to repay you?"

I had a whole lot of questions, but I figured it was probably not the time to ask them. I helped Link pull Mis Crickett out of the coffin and I walked her to the car.

Once we all got home, Mis Crickett immediately sent for Goodic Harken, Dr. Tate, and the police chief, Joe Sullivan. You could have pushed Mr. Harken over with a broom straw when he found out Mis Crickett was alive and well.

Mis Crickett had us all gather in her parlor, where she explained how she'd never really died. Turns out she had a rare brain disorder that made her fall into a catatonic state, appearing to be dead. She had always feared being buried alive, so that's why she'd made such strange requests.

Sipping on hot tea to settle her nerves, Mis Crickett told us that Dr. Tate and Mr. Harken were the only ones who knew the details about her illness, except for her doctors in Nashville. "Dr. Tate, you are a man of honor. I thank you for trying to do the right thing," she said, shaking his hand.

I noticed that Goodie Harken was pacing the floor, back and forth, back and forth. Suddenly he stopped, and, pointing at Link, he shouted, "Arrest this man! It's obvious he's a scoundrel and was up to no good when he dug up our beloved Mis Crickett."

Mis Crickett sat forward in her chair. "You'll do no such thing," she said sternly. "Goodie Harken, I trusted you. You knew that I might still be alive, but all you could think about was getting my money."

"Preposterous!" He snatched up his hat and, with a disgusted huff, stormed out the door.

"I won't be needing your services anymore," Mis Crickett called after him.

By now, Chief Sullivan was completely bewildered. Looking for something to call a crime, he turned to Link. "What made you disturb Mis Crickett's grave, boy?"

Link answered calmly. "I knew she was alive down there."

"She never told you 'bout her illness, so just *how* did you know?"

"I put two and two together and got four. Mis Crickett read us a story one time called 'The Premature Burial' by Edgar Allan Poe," he explained. "I remembered the story well. Scary!"

Link went on. "I figured Mis Crickett had that worry on her mind. The way she'd just shut down sometimes, then come on again. Add the trips to Nashville to see a special doctor. And I heard Mis Crickett say a heap a times, too, that she didn't want to be buried inside a week. She was strong on that point. I figured it had to be for a reason."

"I heard her say it, too," I added.

Link was convincing when he said, "I knew in my heart Mis Crickett was alive! She'd had one of her spells and was down there getting ready to wake up buried. Can you imagine how awful that would be? Buried alive."

Chief Sullivan sighed and shook his head. The idea of such a situation was horrifying. "Well, why didn't you show up at the wake, maybe tell somebody about this?" he asked. "We could have helped."

"Mis Crickett's been like kin to me," Link explained. "When Mr. Harken didn't honor Mis Crickett's wishes, I didn't know what to do. Who would've believed me? So, like a coward, I decided just to leave town. After sitting down by the levee all night thinking—thinking 'bout po' Mis Crickett—I decided come morning to dig her up when no one was around."

"You mean to tell me the jewelry had nothing to do with your disturbing the grave?" Chief Sullivan asked. "What if Mis Crickett really had been dead? Would you have taken the jewelry then?"

Link Murphy never twitched a muscle. "Like I told you, Chief Sullivan, I *knew* Mis Crickett was alive."

The policeman was ready to question Link more, but Mis Crickett raised a finger in the air to stop him. She set her teacup on the table and pulled a shawl over her shoulders. In front of the policeman she took off the diamond earrings, the pearls, and the gold rings she'd been buried in and handed them to Link, saying, "These are yours. Thank you for my life."

Link took the treasure in his hands and caressed the stones one at a time, the way he had the day I caught him holding them. "Thank you, Mis Crickett," he said. "I so love beautiful things," he added, looking straight at her.

Addressing Chief Sullivan, Mis Crickett said, "Now, I think we've settled the matter. I don't want to hear any more about any of this. It's over." She dismissed the chief with an imperial gesture.

Since there wasn't a crime or any proof of criminal intent, the case was officially closed. Of course, the court of public opinion was open and in full session, with plenty of judges.

Those who liked Link said he had done an honorable thing for which he was well rewarded. But others, like Mama, thought differently. "It's as plain as the nose on yo' face," she said. "Link Murphy dug up Mis Crickett to get those jewels!"

Mis Crickett didn't care what people thought. She lived many more years, and kept right on wearing her jewelry. Link drove for her until the day she really died. Then he cashed in the jewels and bought two more cars for his jitney service.

Link Murphy changed houses, cars, and wives with regularity, but he never changed his story. Let him tell it, he *knew* Mis Crickett had been alive. Maybe Mama was right when she claimed Link was a snake and a weasel. Like Mis Crickett, I stopped caring what other people thought. All I know is I enjoyed his company on those summer evenings we all sat together listening to the words of James Whitcomb Riley and Paul Laurence Dunbar.

THE BEST LIE EVER TOLD

Dedicated to my beloved
aunt Nell, who inspired
this story

My uncle by marriage, Kyle Morgan, lived up north, but he came home every summer to visit his folks. That was when he'd stop by and see Mama Frances, who was his sister-in-law. He had lived in the city for many years, but he was as country as they came. He talked country, he walked country, and he dressed real country. Everyone even called him Buddy. Now, how much more country can you get?

Uncle Buddy could tell the best porch lies I ever heard. "You think I'm good at fabricating?" he'd say. "Well, you should have known the legendary Dooley Hunter, who won the state liars' contest five consecutive years—that's in a row—one, two, three, four, five. I was there the day Dooley won his first medal, with a whopper everybody still calls the Best Lie Ever Told."

I always begged to hear that story and Uncle Buddy never let me down. Taking a seat on the top step, he'd remove his hat and commence to talking.

"Back in nineteen and thirty-nine there was a honest-to-goodness liars' contest at the state fair," he'd begin. "In those days, 'lie' was a word we used for a wild or unbelievable story. I'll always remember the year, 'cause it was 'fore baby Lucille was born in 'forty and after sister Cinty got hooked up with that notorious John Henry George in 'thirty-eight. Yes, it was nineteen thirty-nine."

One hot September morning, I went into town to take care of some banking, and I noticed signs were posted everywhere. They were calling for people to come register for the liars' contest at the state fair to be held later in the month. The grand prize was a brand-new John Deere tractor.

I hadn't lived here but a few months, so I was still getting to know all the guys who hung round over at the open-air market. We were forever talking 'bout some of everything but nothing in particular. One day, we were discussing who might do well in the liars' contest, when out of nowhere comes Dooley Hunter loping down the sidewalk, looking for all the world like an oversized toddler.

Dooley was a one-of-a-kind in a one-size-fits-all world. He was slow talking and slow walking, but he had the quickest smile in Davidson County. Nice fellow who always had some wild story to share. Po' Dooley took a lot of ribbing from the guys, who teased him unmercifully 'bout his ridiculous whale whoppers.

Dooley might have been a big ol' country boy in men's shoes, but I suspected there was more to him than met the eye. He reminded me of a fellow I knew over in Memphis by the name of Stanley

Shaker. Everybody tried to take advantage of ol' Stan, mistaking his kindness for stupidity. But them that sold him short soon found out that Stanley might have been simple-looking but he was *not* simpleminded.

"What y'all talkin' 'bout?" Dooley asked, picking his tooth with a straw.

"The liars' contest what's gon' be held at the state fair," I answered. "Winner's gon' drive home a brand-new John Deere tractor."

"I'll say," Dooley mumbled to himself.

"What's that?" I asked.

Speaking up, Dooley says, "You know, I don't reckon I've ever seen a *new* tractor."

Truth be told, none of us had.

"You gon' try to win?" John Tabor asked.

Dooley looked at the notice. "Don't know," he said, digging in the dirt with the toe of his boot.

"Come on, Dooley. It's all for fun," I put in.

"My mama—bless her departed soul—teached me to always tell the truth, and I've honored her memory by always telling the truth."

"Always?" I asked.

"Always," he answered. "You know, every one of my stories happened. I wouldn'ta told 'em if they wasn't so."

"Dooley, sounds like you been living out in the country by yo'self too long," I said, not meaning for it to be funny. Everybody laughed anyhow.

While the other guys were busy poking fun at Dooley, he paid them no mind. He studied the flyer and let his gnarled fingers trace the outline of the tractor. "I sure could use one of these," he said. "Is telling a lie the only way to win?"

"Yes, it is, Dooley," I said. "And the competition is likely to be right smart. You have to convince the judges when you've finished that you've just told the biggest and best whopper of all the contestants."

"Yeah, like that one you just told 'bout never lying," Skeet added.

"But I never . . ."

Though it didn't make an impression on me then, later on I would remember the half-smile on Dooley Hunter's face.

"Come on, enter the contest," I continued, trying to convince him. "Registration for our county is this coming Friday. Give it a try, Dooley. You could use that tractor."

To my surprise, Dooley took Friday off and asked me to go with him to sign up for the state fair liars' contest.

While he and I stood in the registration line minding our own business, one of the other contestants leaned over and asked, "You got a strategy?"

"Never had one of them. Do they get good mileage?" Dooley asked.

At last, me and Dooley came to a young woman who was seated behind a desk. It was Clara Lewis, a round young lady with bright eyes and a voice that sounded like she was singing when she talked.

Porch Lies

She smiled and Dooley looked at her like she was a piece of heaven come down to earth in a gingham dress. He fumbled with his hat and shifted his weight from one foot to the other, while all the time Clara was blushing. "Name? Address?" she asked in her singsong style.

Dooley must've been so taken with Clara that he was struck dumb. I had to answer for him.

When I'd finished, Clara handed Dooley a form to fill out, front and back. "This here is so when the announcer introduces you, he's got something to say," she explained in the key of C. Then she batted her eyelashes and smiled. "I hope you win, Dooley Hunter. Honest I do."

It took Dooley the good part of an hour, but he struggled through the form all the way to the end. He laid the paper on the desk. Clara smiled again, and po' Dooley stopped breathing. I poked him in the side and he sucked in a mouthful of air, sputtering and coughing the way a drowning man gasps for breath.

Clara giggled. She looked over the form, then said sweetly, "You gon' tell a good story?"

"No, ma'am, Mis Clara," he said, grinning, "I aine gon' say much of nothing."

"Much of nothing?" Clara smiled again and winked. "Oh, c'mon, what is it? You can tell me," she whispered. She flashed a big smile, and it sure looked like Dooley was going to spill the beans, but I ribbed him again.

"No, ma'am," he said. "I'm 'fraid you'll have to wait like everybody else, Mis Clara."

She pouted a bit, but I pulled Dooley away 'fore she got it out of him. Even so, Clara rushed off to tell her friend Margaret Jane, who told Cora Lynn, and before long, it was all over the county that Dooley Hunter planned on winning the state liars' contest by saying not "much of nothing."

✕✕✕✕

All the guys down at the open-air market had an opinion about Dooley's "much of nothing" comment. And they freely expressed themselves at their regular spot.

"I hope Dooley's got a plan," said John, guzzling down a big RC.

"What do you s'pose is on his little pea brain?" added Blu Jackson, another one of the guys. "Dooley knows he's got to come up with a doozy to win against the kind of competition he's got."

"I've heard him tell some pretty good yarns with a straight face," I put in. "I'll put my money on him. He'll come up with something."

"Well, I aine so willing to put my neck out there," Skeet Hogan said. "When Dooley makes a fool of himself on that stage, people will think we're all too dumb to tell a good lie here in Davidson County."

Well, they tried to get me to talk Dooley into dropping out of the contest. But he wasn't hearing it. "I'm gon' win," he told me, looking a bit disappointed.

"Yes, but Dooley, you're going to have to do more than say, 'not much of nothing.' "

"You just wait and see."

✕✕✕✕

And so we did. Finally it was the day of the liars' contest, and we were all there. The guys who hung out at the open-air market—Blu

Porch Lies

Jackson, Skeet Hogan, and Kyle Morgan—arrived early, but they sat in the back. Just in case Dooley messed up, they could slip away unnoticed. I didn't care what the others thought. I sat right up front and saved Dooley a seat.

There was a spillover crowd at the tent when Dooley showed up, clean as you please. Had a crease in his overalls, no mud on his shoes, shirt buttoned to his neck, all twenty hairs combed, and every one of his four teeth brushed.

Joe Riley of radio station WMJL was the announcer, and he took the stage amid wild applause. Dooley closed his eyes and cheered.

"Why are your eyes closed?" I asked.

"I always listen to Joe Riley. It's hard for me to listen and look at him at the same time."

Joe Riley introduced the six judges, and the contest began. The first lying contestant was Forrest Jackman from Watertown in Marion County. He told a fish tale. You know, the one about the big fish that got away. Very predictable.

"Once I catched a catfish down in the bottom," Dooley whispered to me. "Thing was so big, I ate off it for three days." He shook his head. "And that's the truth, 'cept nobody ever believed me when I told 'em." Somebody shushed him and he had to be quiet.

Then a man from up in Summit County unraveled a yarn about Old Smokum, a bear that could count money and make change. It was a good lie. Good enough to win? Maybe.

I looked over at Dooley. He smiled. "Funny thing, a bear once came in my house, sat down to the table, and ate pancakes like a man, then got up, wiped his mouth with a napkin, and left out the back door," he whispered to me. "Nobody ever believed that one, either."

"Really?" I said, thinking, *Maybe Dooley is going to do fine in this contest.*

Next Thomas Bowman from over in Monroe County told a story. "One day I skipped school to go fishing," he began. "But I met a talking snake on the way. 'My name is Coach Whip,' the snake said.

"'Why you call yo'self such a name?' I asked.

"And the snake say, ''Cause I whups little boys what skips school.'"

According to Thomas, ol' Coach Whip raised up and went to chasing him on two feet. And when that snake caught Thomas, it wrapped itself around the boy and commenced to giving him a good spanking.

"I promised that snake I would never miss school again if he just let me go," said Thomas. "And that's why I went to school every day unless I had a good reason not to. I didn't want to get on the bad side of ol' Coach Whip ever again. The end!"

The audience cheered and applauded wildly for Thomas Bowman's tale. The judges looked pleased, too. Thomas had told a downright funny lie.

Dooley's mouth was hanging open in amazement.

"Dooley, are you nervous?" I asked.

"Naw," he said. "I was just thinking 'bout a snake that chased me one time, too. Could have sworn that thing had legs, 'cause it was moving so fast. Wonder if that was ol' Coach Whip."

"Dooley, that was a whopper Thomas told! Snakes can't talk, and they aine got feet, either."

"Snakes do talk. We jus' can't understand their language," he said matter-of-factly. "Besides, I said the snake that chased me moved upright as if it was running on legs."

Porch Lies

I didn't want to get into a discussion with Dooley about talking and running snakes, so I just looked at the stage.

Up next was a woman from Jackson County. She and Joe Riley chitchatted about her prize hens and her fine rooster named Schuster for a minute or two. Then she told a dandy 'bout Schuster dancing the flamenco with a pig named Squeal. She had us all laughing ourselves silly.

When the applause died down, Dooley leaned over to me and whispered, "I ever tell you 'bout that rooster I once had, could tell time good as any clock? He was a fire alarm, too. Saved me from a fire one night."

"Not now," I said.

But Dooley went right into his favorite story about his rooster. "Nobody believed that Wonder Boy was special. They said I imagined it all. But he was a good rooster till that fox got him. Ate him clean up—no feathers, no bones, no nothing left over."

He got shushed again. I punched Dooley with my elbow, and he swallowed his words.

The next liar came up with a ghost story that made my toes curl under. He ended his lie with a big "I gotcha!"

People screamed, jumped out of their seats, and grabbed the folks next to them. "Whoa! That was a good one," I said.

"I'll be right back," Dooley said, and slipped away.

By the time Dooley got back with a bag of peanuts, a corn dog, and a big RC and settled in his seat, Joe Riley was welcoming Junior Meddles from Lippincott County to the stage.

"Let's give Junior a big state fair welcome, " Joe said in his best radio voice.

Well, Junior Meddles's yarn took off in the direction of a dog story, but twenty minutes later, the dog had changed to a horse, and nobody knew what he was talking 'bout. When he finally sat down, the crowd sent up a cheer of relief, and that's what woke the judges.

The audience suffered through three or four more bad contestants, and by then, people were getting a little tired and unruly. Joe Riley held up his hands to gain control. "I know you're restless, folks, but we have one more liar to go. Come on up here, Dooley Hunter from Davidson County." Dooley took a deep breath and eased up onstage like he was climbing the gallows.

I seemed to be the only person from Davidson County who was cheering. I really whooped it up, whistling and hollering. "I'm behind you, Dooley," I shouted, figuring he had as much chance to win as any of the others.

"I see you brought along *a* friend," said Joe Riley. Everybody laughed. I tried not to think of what might happen if Dooley did something really dumb. The boys at the open-air market would never let him forget it, and they'd tease me about being silly enough to support him.

I swallowed hard as Dooley stumbled to center stage. Joe put his hand on Dooley's shoulder. "Tell me, Mr. Hunter," he said, but Dooley cut him off.

"No, sir," he whispered softly, but the mike picked it up. "Mr. Hunter is my daddy. I'm Dooley."

Everybody whooped as Joe rolled his eyes. Then he looked at the form Dooley had filled out when he registered. "It says here, Dooley, if'n you win the tractor you gon' get rid of Dempsey. Now just who is Dempsey?" He stuck the microphone in Dooley's face. It squeaked.

Dooley's eyes looked like a deer's in headlights. "My mule."

A flutter of giggles swept over the crowd.

"If'n I was to win that there tractor as you says, I'm gon' get from behind Dempsey. Then maybe, I'm thinking, I could buy forty or fifty more acres, add to my farm."

People got quiet. Listened, 'cause Dooley was speaking from his heart—simple speech, but wasn't a soul there who couldn't relate to what he was saying. We all had dreams.

"With that tractor," Dooley explained, "I could produce more. Make more money . . . and then maybe get hitched." He looked down at Clara Lewis, who was sitting in the third row center, just a-smiling up at Dooley like he was Prince Somebody of Someplace Wonderful.

"Well, it 'pears you've got it all planned out," Joe Riley said, busting up the magic in that moment. Taking the microphone out of Dooley's hand, he continued. "Are you sure you can win this contest with saying—as you put it—'*not much of nothing*'?"

"Get on with it," a man in the audience yelled.

"Dooley," said the announcer with a big showman's smile, "are you ready to tell us your lie?"

Dooley cleared his throat. "I'm ready."

Joe put the mike on the stand and stood Dooley in front of it. "Then jump right in!"

Dooley started to speak, but the microphone squeaked again and squawked. People sniggled and giggled some more. Dooley looked like a lump on a log.

"Say something," I whispered loudly.

"I'm with you, Dooley!" shouted Clara Lewis.

Porch Lies

As if shocked out of his daze, Dooley looked right at Clara and said in a loud voice, "I aine never told no lie before." And he stepped away from the microphone.

The tent full of noisy people fell silent. Every eye was on Dooley Hunter.

I aine never told no lie before.

That was it?

"Is that it?" Joe Riley asked, looking surprised.

"That's it," Dooley answered.

Suddenly Skeet in the back of the room leaped to his feet. "That's a lie, Dooley Hunter, and you know it! You remember that time you told me that story 'bout a dog you had that could make a fire in the fireplace like a natural-born man? Now, you know that was a great big lie!"

"That lie you just told is the biggest, fattest prevarication I've ever heard!" shouted a woman.

"Well, whatever that word means, I agree if it means it's the biggest, fattest fib ever told," shouted a man up front.

"You can't expect us to believe . . ."

Just then, from the back of the room, someone started clapping. Others joined in, and the sound grew louder and louder until it built to a thundering roar. And the guys from the open-air market were clapping the loudest of all, as it dawned on every one of us what Dooley had done.

Meanwhile, Dooley stood there in the middle of the stage, hat in hand, looking for all the world like the cat that ate the rat.

It was a unanimous decision in nineteen and thirty-nine. Dooley Hunter won the liars' contest hands down.

"You did in one single sentence what all the others weren't able to do no matter how long they went on: tell the best lie," said Joe Riley. Then Dooley got the keys to the new tractor, presented by Miss Tennessee herself.

And that's how our very own Dooley Hunter became a celebrity. Camera lights flashed in his face. People rushed up to shake his hand, but Clara pushed her way to the front and planted a kiss right on his cheek. Now, could life get any sweeter than that?

Later that night, while driving home alone, I smiled because a good thing had happened to a nice guy. "Dooley really did it," I told the moon. " 'I aine never told a lie before.' " I repeated it to myself and laughed again.

But like a growing thirst, an idea began to nag at me. I remembered something—something Dooley had said the day we all encouraged him to sign up for the contest. *"I always tell the truth"* is what he'd said. *"Always."*

I pulled the car over to let the idea really take shape. "Was Dooley playing with us?" I asked a rabbit scampering across the road.

For as long as everybody's known Dooley Hunter, we thought he was fibbing when he told stories about pancake-eating bears, fire-building dogs, and roosters that told time. The stories sounded so incredible, we simply took them to be lies. "But what if," I asked a nightowl perched in a nearby tree, "what if all the time Dooley was actually telling the truth?"

THE EARTH BONE AND THE KING OF THE GHOSTS

Dedicated to the memory
of Lucious Webb, who gave
me my first Earth Bone

Before they moved to the old homestead,
*my grandparents had rented a small shotgun house at 988 Carter Street.
Later they bought the house and rented it out to a man named Lenny
Bowen, Sr.*

*Mr. Lenny had lived in north Nashville all his life, and Mama
Frances considered him a good tenant. I loved it when he stopped by to
pay the rent because he told wonderful "gotcha" stories that made us
jump and holler.*

*One of my favorites was a wonderful porch lie about how a famous
slickster named Montgomery Red came to own a house at 606 Rosehill.
"I lived in the house next door," Lenny would say, "back when I was just
a boy.*

*"You think Stagelee was rough?" he would go on. "You think Big Billy
DeLyon was tough? Let me tell you 'bout Montgomery Red."*

*Then he would take a seat, hitch up his pant legs, and continue the
tale. "Red was so bad he dared to take on the King of the Ghosts. . . ."*

It all started when an unsuspecting real estate agent named Wily Hancock bought a piece of property in the black part of town known as Shotgun Alley. It was called that 'cause all the houses had three rooms that were lined up one behind the other like the barrel of a shotgun. You could stand in the front door and shoot a bullet straight out the back.

Most of the houses were well kept and neat, but the one Wily bought—number 606—was empty and run-down. See, nobody had lived in it for years, and nobody wanted to, either. To put it plain and simple, the place was haunted. From what I'd heard, the haints of number 606 were the scariest in the world.

So Wily was forced to rent the house cheap. Finally, he found a couple who tried to live in it, but they could only take it a week. They fled in the middle of the night, raving about how they'd been attacked by all manner of ghostly creatures.

Next, he rented the place to an elderly couple who hadn't heard about the ghost situation. They moved out after spending one night there and refused to talk about what they'd experienced.

The last family—who'd just shown up from the next town over—walked in the front door and straight out the back, never to return.

Needless to say, it wasn't easy to rent a house that was haunted. Wily had a lemon on his hands, no doubt about it. He couldn't rent it; he couldn't sell it; in fact, he couldn't even give it away.

Or could he?

Wily came up with an idea to advertise in area newspapers that he'd *make a gift* of his house to anybody who could stay in it for three consecutive nights. Each candidate had to put up a hundred-dollar nonrefundable registration fee. At least Wily could recover some of his investment, he figured.

A young man from Steelville took the challenge first. He put up his hundred dollars . . . and he lasted in number 606 for two hours. The last I heard, he was still running.

Next, a bricklayer from over in Monroe County paid his hundred dollars. An ambulance took him away screaming. They tell me that po' soul is wrapping string these days over at the state home.

Montgomery Red just happened to be passing through town when he heard people talking down at the greasy spoon.

It was easy to see how Red got his name. His skin and hair were the same rusty color as the red clay soil of Alabama. His high cheekbones, prominent nose, and light brown eyes indicated he was an Afro–Native American blend.

"That place is haunted by the King of the Ghosts," one of the locals was saying. "Can't nobody stay in it."

That got Red's attention. "What house?" he asked, slurping his coffee and polishing off his third donut.

People were more than willing to tell the big stranger about 606 Rosehill Avenue and how its owner was willing to give it away.

Before anybody knew it, Red had signed the papers and paid his hundred-dollar nonrefundable registration fee. Word spread like wildfire. Big, bad Montgomery Red was gon' face the King of the Ghosts.

I met Montgomery Red when I rode my bicycle past the empty house next door on my way to the corner store for Mama. He was on his knees searching the ground, looking for something. "Hi. I'm Lenny Bowen. Can I help you, sir?" I asked.

"Well, well, you are a real gentleman. Pleased to meet you," Big Red said to me, smiling. "Call me Red." We shook hands and a friendship began instantly.

"You really going in that house over there?" I asked, having already heard about him.

"Yep!"

I gasped, not looking at the windows too long for fear of what I might see. "Why?"

"Time for me to settle down," Red said, sighing. "This seems like as good a place as any." He got back to his searching.

"Right now, I'm looking for an Earth Bone," he threw in matter-of-factly. "You seen one?"

"No, sir," I answered, backing up a piece, just in case an Earth Bone was dangerous. "I aine even now heard of no such thing."

Red shook his head. "Boy, how you get to be however old you are and not know 'bout an Earth Bone?"

I mumbled something 'bout if it had anything to do with conjure, my folks wouldn't approve.

Suddenly Red stood up so tall I thought he'd never unwind. Why, he had to be well over six four. He cradled something in his huge hand. "Am I lucky to have found this!" He chuckled. "Now I'm as bad as any ghosts in that house."

"May—may I see it?" I asked, marveling at the idea that something so powerful existed. "What's it do?"

In his palm lay the Earth Bone. It looked like an ordinary rock, but I didn't want to 'pear ignorant, so I kept still.

"With this," Red explained, "I don't have to be scared of nothing that creeps, crawls, slithers, slides, or goes bump in the night. I can stop all ghosts, ghouls, and monsters in their tracks."

Porch Lies

As Red turned to go into the house, a knot formed in my stomach. Even with the Earth Bone, I wondered, did he really have a chance?

I wished my new friend well. "It would have been nice having you as a neighbor," I said, and waved good-bye.

Now, what happened when Montgomery Red entered number 606 is just what he says happened. If it's a lie, then it's the lie he told.

Say Red brushed his teeth, put on his pajamas, and hopped into bed. Before he could speak the words, *Hiss-be-quiggle-dee-dum-dee-dum*, he was in a deep sleep. Didn't know how long, but he woke up, sensing that somebody or something was in the room along with him. Problem was, it was inky dark and impossible to know for sure.

Suddenly he heard talking in the blackness.

"He's mine," whispered a scratchy voice.

"No, he's mine," another voice hissed.

"Looks tough to me," said the first.

"I brought along the hot sauce."

"Good! Let's split him down the middle. You eat one side, I'll eat the other."

That was when Red grabbed his flashlight and switched it on. Framed in the circle of light sat two of the biggest, ugliest ghost pirates you could imagine. And what was in front of them, waiting to be cut in two? Nothing but a big fried catfish.

Was Red petrified? He never said. All I know is what he told me, and I'm telling you.

Red shouted to get their attention. "Hey! Hey! Hey! I wish y'all would take that noise elsewhere. Can't you see I'm trying to sleep?"

The ghost pirates fell speechless. They looked at Red with surprised, red-rimmed eyes.

"Boooooo!" one of the ghosts wailed pathetically.

Red held up the charm. "Watch out, I've got an Earth Bone, and if you come near me, I'm gon' use it!"

"What's an Earth Bone?" the first pirate asked the other.

"Must be powerful, 'cause look, he aine one bit a-scared of us," the second pirate answered.

"Go on." Red ordered them out of the room. "I have work to do tomorrow and need my sleep. Git!"

The ghost pirates' faces sagged with disappointment as they floated out the door like naughty children. But the first pirate called over his shoulder, "Aye, you may not be a-scared of *us*, but you wait till Ralph comes."

"Who's Ralph?" Red asked.

"He's the *King* of the Ghosts," the second pirate replied. "And this is *his* house."

Red burst out laughing. "You go tell ol' Ralph that my name is Montgomery Red and this is *my* house." And Red pulled the covers up over his head, and before he knew it, dawn had come.

✕✕✕✕✕

Imagine how I felt when come first light I found Big Red on the front porch whistling. He tilted his head toward two paintbrushes and a can of white paint. "Glad to see you, li'l' buddy."

Taking up a brush, I couldn't wait to ask, "Did you see any ghosties?"

"Just two," Red answered. Then he told me all about what had happened during the night.

"So the Earth Bone took care of 'em, huh?"

"Seems so."

As word spread that Montgomery Red had survived a full night at number 606 and was painting the place, people began gathering to see what manner of man this was—including Wily.

Red was now the closest thing to a celebrity we'd ever had in Shotgun Alley. He had stayed in a ghost house all night and was still around to tell about it.

Even though many well wishes were extended that day, not one person stayed after sunset. As soon as darkness fell, Montgomery Red was alone at 606.

Getting ready for bed that night, I felt special that my new friend had shared the secret of his strength with me. An Earth Bone! And I lay awake half the night wondering how Red was faring against the King of the Ghosts.

Meanwhile, somewhere in a place between here and there, a clock struck two in the morning. Red say he woke up. The battery in his flashlight was dead, so he calmly lit a candle and looked around the room. Nobody to be seen. But an invisible hand began to write big bloody letters on the wall.

B G I T M

Red waited until the writing stopped. "I've never seen that word before," he said to the writer. "Explain yo'self."

A gust of wind flung open the door to the bedroom. It swirled and twisted and blew things off the table. The window swung open, and a terrible, booming voice bellowed, "It means *Be Gone In The Morning.*"

Was Red scared? If you guessed no, you'd be right.

"I've got an Earth Bone, and everybody knows what it can do to a ghost. Are you sure you're big and bad enough to make me leave?" he challenged the phantom.

"Ralph's ON HIS WAY!" came the answer. Then in a flash the windy ghost swooped off and the door and the window slammed shut.

Everything was still and quiet—a little too quiet. Red fell back on the pillow and waited. Slowly, in front of his eyes, a woman materialized at the foot of the bed. She was holding her head in her outstretched hands.

And the head spoke.

"Ralph sent me to tell you to leave *his* house. If I were you, I'd git to steppin'—*now!*" Then the headless woman vanished.

"You got to do better than that to scare me!" Red scoffed, paying no attention to the twenty sets of ghostly eyes that were watching and blinking in wonder and surprise outside his window. "I aine scared of y'all, long as I got my Earth Bone." With that, Montgomery Red rolled over in bed and went back to sleep!

Porch Lies

Morning came, and half the town, including me, cheered mightily as Red emerged from 606 unscathed. Within an hour, a truckload of men had showed up with hoes, shovels, and rakes, and they set to cleaning the yard, clearing away years of overgrown bushes and hedges. I helped.

But not one of us set foot inside that house.

By noon, a group of women had put together enough lunch to feed us all with leftovers to spare. Sadie Louise, my big sister, was so impressed with Red, she giggled like a six-year-old in a candy store when he winked at her; Mama saw it, and gave her the eye. It tickled me—the idea of Sadie Louise and Montgomery Red.

At sunset, and for the third time, we all left Red alone.

"You still got the Earth Bone?" I whispered 'fore I took off.

Red took it out of his pocket and showed it to me. For all the world it looked like an ordinary rock. But I knew this had to be something very, very powerful.

Red told me later that he did his nightly routine and turned in early. He was sleeping soundly when all of a sudden his bed began to shake. The room grew colder and colder still, until it felt like the inside of an icehouse. He could see clouds of breath coming from his nose and mouth. As a strange, otherworldly white light flooded the room, the door burst open, and there in the doorway stood a grotesque blob of horror.

"Dinnertime!" it roared.

Red stood his ground.

"I'm Ralph, King of the Ghosts, and I've come to gobble you up and spit out the skin and bones." Ralph roared and squeaked and squealed and barked all at the same time.

Red didn't flinch. "I think it's fair to warn you that I've got an Earth Bone, and if you know what's good for you, *you'll* leave before it's too late. . . ."

"What is that thing? Give it to me." Ralph grabbed for the Earth Bone, but Red was too fast. He sidestepped the big monster ghost and tripped him as the ghost lunged forward.

Splat! Ralph fell flat on his face and broke into hundreds of little Ralphs. All of them quickly rushed toward Red, but he held out the Earth Bone and began to chant:

> "A google de-goop,
> De-moop,
> De-loop."

The little Ralphs scattered. From behind curtains, under tables, and between books, they shouted, "Hold on! Stop that chanting! What are you doing?"

"You've given me no choice," said Red. "I'm getting ready to finish the spell, and when I do, it's gon' be all over for you."

Ralph quickly pulled himself together again, then snatched at the Earth Bone. But he couldn't get hold of it.

Red went on chanting:

> "A google de-goop,
> De-moop,
> De-loop."

Ralph howled and moaned. "Stop! Don't! What do you want?"

"Well, first," said Red, "can't you do something 'bout the way you look? And warm it up a bit in here?"

Ralph began to quiver and glow as he shape-shifted into a large black cat. "Will this do?"

"Is that you, Ralph, King of the Ghosts?" Red asked, feeling warmer at the same time.

"It's me," the ghost answered in a whiny voice. Big Red stroked Ralph's head as the cat shared his hard-luck story. "I've lived here a long, long time," he wailed. "If you make me leave, I'll have no place to go. Neither will my friends. Please don't make us go."

Red thought about it. "Tell you what," he said. "If y'all promise to do 'way with the horror show and let me sleep at night, you can stay in my house."

The cat arched his back and hissed angrily. "*Me?* Live with *you*? I think not. I am King of the Ghosts! This is my house. I will allow *you* to live with *me.*"

Red wiggled the Earth Bone in Ralph's face.

"Mercy!" Ralph wailed, accepting defeat. "Okay, on your terms, but can't we at least have the others think the house is still mine? Pretty please? I do have a reputation to maintain."

Red shrugged. "King of the Ghosts, you've made yourself a deal."

And that's how the three-day war between Montgomery Red and the King of the Ghosts ended with no casualties.

✕✕✕✕✕

I was there that morning when Red came out of 606, carrying a big, black, green-eyed cat. It never occurred to any of us that he was

holding the King of the Ghosts. And amid great fanfare and all the publicity he could wring out of it, Wily deeded the house to Montgomery Red, while the cat looked on.

Later, when Red had time, he told me about Ralph's agreement that all the ghosts at number 606 would live as cats.

"You gon' stay there, surrounded by all them haints and such?" I asked.

"They're harmless, long as I have my Earth Bone," he answered.

We couldn't help but laugh, watching the lot of them licking their paws, sunning on the railing, and batting at sunbeams.

My curiosity got the best of me and I asked with wide eyes, "Mr. Red, may I see the Earth Bone again?"

"I'll do you one better," he answered, "if you tell that pretty sister of yours I said hi."

I agreed quickly, and Red reached down and picked up a common, everyday, ordinary rock. "Here's an Earth Bone all yo' own," he said, and tossed it to me. And a fresh grin crinkled up his face as he walked into his new home.

CAKE NORRIS LIVES ON
PART ONE

Dedicated to Erma Carwell, my mom,
who told us stories about her
father, whose nickname was Cake

Uncle George, my grandfather's brother, *visited every second Sunday. After an early supper, we'd sit around and tell stories. Uncle George told wonderful tales about Noble "Cake" Norris, who, according to my uncle, was the very first blues harmonica player in the world. "Everybody who knew Cake wondered why a man with that much talent wasted so much of his time being a prankster. He just couldn't pass up a dare," said Uncle George. "Cake ran toward anything wild and crazy like a moth to flame. It proved to be his undoing."*

But did Cake take a dare and dive off the Cumberland Bridge, as some say? Or did he fall off it accidentally in a snowstorm? Or was he pushed? When? Where? How? "Who knows what happened to him," said Uncle George. "Somebody counted one time, and came up with twenty-seven ways Cake was supposed to have died. Then there's some of us who don't believe Cake Norris is really dead."

Porch Lies

When we kids asked why not, Uncle George would smile and say, "You don't want to hear that old porch lie again, do you?"

Although I'd listened to it at least twenty times, I never tired of being told about my favorite slickster-trickster. Even today when I hear the wail of a harmonica, I hear my great-uncle's raspy voice beginning a yarn about the immortal Cake Norris.

XXXXX

Say Noble Norris was a self-taught musician—the first to perfect the blues harmonica. None better in the world, I tell you! He was so good, even Death let him slide—or so the story goes.

His nickname was Cake 'cause he loved the two-egg puddings his mama baked. She'd turn them out on a rack to cool, but by the time she got around to spreading on the icing, her son would have already nibbled away half of the thing. And so she went to calling him Cake. The name stuck. So did the habit of being a rascal.

Cake was a restless soul drawn to danger for the thrill of it. The more exciting or frightening an adventure was, the more he loved it.

But as devilish as he was, there was also something likable about Cake. He was good-natured; never held a grudge—would give away the shirt on his back. He loved to have fun—eating, singing, telling stories. Oh, but when he picked up that harmonica and commenced to playing, men stopped working, women's hands got still, little children fell quiet, and they all listened.

One day, Cake left home and never came back. One story says he died trying to break a wild horse over in Abilene, Texas. Another story details how Cake got in a watermelon-eating contest and ate six whole melons and his stomach burst. And there's even one so-called eyewitness account that said Cake was taken out while wrestling an alligator in a carnival sideshow in Jefferson City, Missouri. N'er a word of it is true.

Anyway, it's safe to say that one day Cake Norris woke up dead.

There he was standing before the Pearly Gates, and they were every bit as beautiful as he'd heard. Truth be told, he was somewhat surprised to be there. After all, he knew what folks were bound to put on his tombstone:

HERE LIES NOBLE "CAKE" NORRIS.
THE DEVIL DON'T WANT HIM
AND HEAVEN AINE READY FOR HIM.

Cake anxiously rang the doorbell. When nobody answered, he laid on the buzzer louder and longer.

"Okay, okay, I'm comin'," he heard from the other side, then keys rattling, followed by a big clank. He stepped back as the doors slowly creaked open. "State yo' business," a tall black angel said, looking at him over the rim of his glasses.

"Don't I know you?" Cake asked. "Didn't we meet at a rent party up in Harlem?"

"I think not!" huffed the angel with a pompous sneer.

"Okay. But could you tell me something? Am I dead?"

"Forevermore," the angel replied in a no-nonsense voice. Humorless!

"Are you the one they call Saint Peter?" Cake wanted to know. He peered over the angel's head to see inside.

"No, I'm Roscoe, one of Saint Peter's assistants," the angel

answered, stepping out onto a cloud and closing the gate behind him. "Saint Peter is away on business at the north gate. This here is the south gate."

"Are you gon' let me in?"

"Name?"

"Cake Norris."

Roscoe leafed through a notebook, all the time mumbling. "Nathan, Nemo, Nissen, Nowell. Nope. No Norris. Your name is not listed," he said matter-of-fact-like. "You can't get in 'less'n you listed in the Book of Names."

"Look again," Cake pleaded.

Roscoe sighed, then reluctantly searched the book once more. "I see no Cake Norris," he said, taking out a magnifying glass. "No, now wait . . . I've got a Noble James Norris, Junior, here on the last page at the bottom, written in teeny-tiny print." He gave Cake a disgusted smirk.

"That's me!" Cake pointed to himself. "I'm in the book! I made it! Look out, heaven, here I come!" And he hurried toward the Pearly Gates.

But Roscoe held up a hand. "Hold on one minute, there. You can't just come running up in here. You're on the last page, at the very bottom, in print so small I need a magnifying glass to read it. The bottom!" Roscoe added for emphasis.

"So? I'm in the book," Cake said, looking bewildered.

"You're borderline," Roscoe explained. "Not bad enough, not good enough. You're in between, which means you must go to a holding station."

Cake looked longingly at the Pearly Gates.

Meanwhile, Roscoe was hastily thumbing through another book

called *Station Assignments.* "Okay. We're gon' start you out on station seventy-five," he said.

"Is that bad or good?"

Roscoe peered over the top of his glasses. "This is how it works around here. Listen carefully, 'cause I'll not repeat it. There are ninety-nine stations between heaven and . . . down there. Reach ninety-nine and you march through the Pearly Gates. All stations over fifty are upward bound. All stations under fifty are going the other way. Reach number one and you go . . . well, you know. Do you catch my drift?"

"Yes, sir."

"If you keep your mouth shut and your nose clean and stay out of trouble, you'll advance rather quickly," Roscoe went on. "But misbehave and I'll have to bust you down. If you get busted below station fifty, then you're out of my jurisdiction. Got it?"

"Got it," said Cake.

Roscoe snapped his fingers. An elevator appeared and Cake stepped on behind the angel.

Inside there were buttons numbered from zero to ninety-nine, and Roscoe pressed seventy-five.

The zero button was red and flashing, and Cake reached over to inspect it.

Roscoe gasped in horror. "Don't touch *that*!"

Just then the elevator doors opened and a woman's voice and a big sign greeted Cake as he stepped out.

WELCOME TO STATION 75.
WATCH YOUR STEP.

"Keep that in mind," said Roscoe. "Every day I'm gon' be watchin' just how you steppin'. So behave."

The doors shut, and the elevator vanished. Cake was left to explore his new surroundings. Everything was operating-room fresh and clean without the smell of disinfectant. Every house was painted and each yard was bursting with blooms. It reminded Cake of where he'd lived as a child.

As Cake walked along he began to play his harmonica. People recognized the sound. "Cake Norris is up here," said one man. Soon people began to gather. Seems a lot of his friends and neighbors were at this station. He greeted each one with a big smile and a hug.

"Well, sir," Sister Honeywell said, teasing. "Imagine the likes of you getting this close to Glory."

Cake took off his hat respectfully. "Sister Honeywell, I'm shocked that you only got this far. I thought the way you shouted on Sunday morning they'd a let you run through the Pearly Gates."

Sister Honeywell blushed and went to fanning herself with a church fan. "Chile, it wasn't what I did on Sunday, but what I did on Saturday landed me here."

"We did have some fun times playing cards, didn't we all?" said Cake.

Sister Honeywell closed her eyes and sighed. "I got a lot of memories from back then." Then she caught herself. "Get 'way from me, Cake Norris. Making me remember all those shameful times in my life. You'll get me busted."

"Sorry," he said to Sister Honeywell as he continued exploring.

Out of nowhere, Cake heard singing. It sounded familiar. As he drew closer, who did he find but Mitchell and Michael O'Brian, two gospel-singing twins he'd known since childhood.

"Well, if it aine Cake Norris," said Mitchell, smiling broadly. "I heard you were here. Somebody say they heard you playing your harmonica."

Cake smiled back, then asked, "Why in the world are y'all in a holding station? You two sang more people into glory than most preachers."

Mitchell explained. "Before we switched to gospel, we sang in blues joints, dance halls, gambling dens, anywhere we could make a dime."

"And that's how come we here," Michael added. "But we're trying to move on up a little higher, if you know what I mean."

The brothers said they were in charge of the station choir, and Michael suggested that Cake join.

"I remember when you sang in the Mount Olive junior choir," Mitchell said.

"That was a dog's age," said Cake. He chuckled and shook his head as if thinking about something from long ago and far, far away. "Yes. I'd like to join the choir."

And so Cake made himself at home on station seventy-five.

The first day he showed up for choir practice there was trouble. He took one look at the white robes and laughed so hard, he broke a sweat. "Man, where'd y'all get these from? Didn't we see enough white robes on Klansmen never to want to see another one?"

"I hadn't even thought . . . I s'pose you're right," mumbled Michael, and all the choir members nodded.

"When we get to heaven gon' put on our robes, and they

aine gon' be white, neither," they started to sing in four-part harmony. The O'Brian brothers agreed, and all of them removed their robes.

The organist put in that they should take up a collection to buy new choir robes. Mitchell passed the hat and each member made a donation. Then they handed Cake the money and gave him the job of selecting the robes.

"Is this going to be enough?" Cake asked.

"Around here, whatever you have is enough," said Mitchell.

So the next day Cake went to the commissary and picked out bright red robes. He brought them to choir rehearsal that evening, and he handed one to each choir member.

"Looka here. Looka here," said Mitchell, putting his on and strutting around.

"I haven't seen nothing this pretty since the A.M.E. annual conference in 'thirty-five," Michael added.

Cake started singing "The Old Ship of Zion," and a gospel songfest began.

By evening some of the choir members from South Carolina had formed a circle and broken out in a ring shout. The stomping and clapping had grown so loud, holding station seventy-five was shaking on its very foundation.

Some of the pious souls were scandalized by it all. "Red is such a vulgar color," they whispered.

"We like our red robes," countered Mitchell.

"And we're not giving them up," added Michael.

Well, they bickered back and forth and back again, till Mitchell suggested taking the matter to Roscoe.

"We have a situation!" reported Mitchell, and he filled the angel in on their dispute.

"I can't have this kind of confusion going on at one of my stations," Roscoe said between gritted teeth.

"We aine wearin' no white robes," the brothers argued.

"Well, you aine gon' wear red robes, neither!" Roscoe said emphatically.

Roscoe scratched his head, studying on the situation. At last he shouted, "Blue robes. That's it! Blue robes only. They'll blend in better with the clouds and sky."

Mitchell and Michael were pleased. So were the choir members. And all those who objected to the red robes were appeased. Joyfully the matter was settled.

But Roscoe blamed the whole mess on Cake. "I'm taking you down a notch, mister!" he declared.

Instantly, Cake found himself on station seventy.

"I was only trying to help," he whined.

"You'd better watch your step!" Roscoe said from above.

For a while, Cake managed not to be noticed on station seventy. To calm his spirit, he sat under a large shade tree and played his harmonica. A few people there remembered the sound—where they'd been and who they'd been with when they'd first heard that soulful music. "It must be Cake Norris," they said. For some the music made them sad. Others smiled. But most just shut their eyes and listened.

Within a day or two, Cake had learned the lay of the land. And by the end of the week, he was on the wrong side of a half-dozen visiting cherubs. He teased the po' li'l' angels something awful, chasing them in and around the clouds, tickling their tiny feet, and hiding their halos. They must've reminded him of the children who lived in his old neighborhood. He even twisted their angel wings, so that when they took off, they flew upside down.

Wasn't long 'fore a cluster of them fluttered over to log a complaint with Roscoe.

"You're calling attention to yo'self," Roscoe told Cake, pulling him aside. "Now you've got two strikes against you, so I've got to bust you down to station sixty. Best be careful."

Cake stayed out of trouble for a few weeks, but by month's end, he had hidden Zeus's thunderbolts, gotten caught playing on Apollo's golden harp, and tricked the Sandman out of his sack so that nobody could get to sleep for three days.

After reading the many, many anti-Cake complaints on his desk, Roscoe was fuming. "I just knew you were trouble when I saw you was on the last page of the Book of Names. Cake Norris, you're busted to station fifty," he ordered. "Yo' last chance. Stop being so devilish . . . or else!"

✕✕✕✕✕

Things went along smoothly on station fifty until Cake got the bright idea to have a fish fry. They say it was an affair to remember. He served up fresh catfish caught in the river Jordan. Had slaw, potato salad, sliced tomatoes and onions, hush puppies, and his favorite—warm cake—for dessert. Everybody who was anybody was there.

"Come on in, Big O and Li'l' I," Cake said, welcoming none other than Osiris, Egyptian King of the Dead, and his lovely wife, Isis, to the party. She was as beautiful as ever and he was his usual somber self.

After the feast, there was a story swap. Cake took the stage and told a notorious porch lie, had everybody rolling on the floor. Even Osiris had to smile, and that was really stretching it for him. Then Cake played his harmonica and the music was so lively that some folk almost forgot where they were. Had to hold their feet to keep from getting carried away.

The party went on until Roscoe returned from duty on the north gate and got a whiff of fish grease. He followed it to the source. Hearing the lively music, he turned the party out and sent everybody home. "Cake, you can't throw parties and play music like this was a juke joint. That's three strikes now, and you're out!"

"All I was trying to do was have a little fun."

"That's part of the problem," Roscoe scolded, picking up the telephone. "This is serious business here."

Someone must've answered on the other end, because Roscoe said, "Hello. We got a reject from holding station fifty. Just aine good enough. I'm sending him to you right now."

Suddenly, the elevator materialized and the doors opened. Cake stepped on and closed his eyes. Roscoe pressed a button. And the elevator began to fall.

CAKE NORRIS LIVES ON

PART TWO

Dedicated to my children
and grandchildren with the
hope that they will always
remember our family stories
and tell them

Mama would say it was time for bed, but
*all us kids would beg to hear the rest of the story. Uncle George acted like
he didn't know what we were talking about. "What rest of the story?"*

*"Tell us what happened when the elevator went down, pretty please?"
I'd beg.*

*Uncle George would claim he'd forgotten that part. But we knew better. Finally, when Mama had been coaxed into letting us stay up and we
couldn't stand to wait another minute, Uncle George would smile, lean
back, and pick up the tale. . . .*

Po' Cake rode that elevator down, down, down, down, past station
forty-five. Down, down some more. Past station forty. "Oh, no,"
Cake cried. Down the elevator dropped. On past station thirty.

Porch Lies

Then the elevator slowed down, passing stations twenty-nine, twenty-seven, twenty-six.

Clank! At station twenty-five, the elevator came to a dead stop. The doors flung open, and Cake found himself standing on the banks of the dreaded Deep River. On the far shore a huge red neon sign was flashing, and a woman's sultry voice announced: "Welcome to station twenty-five—you're on your way!"

The elevator vanished, but not before Cake heard Roscoe's voice call out from above, "You're on your way, a'right!"

"To where?" Cake asked.

"You'll find out."

Now Cake was alone. He looked for something good to hang hope on. *At least Roscoe didn't press the zero button*, he thought, his head drooping.

He looked around. What to do? What to do? Layers of darkness covered the place like musty old blankets, even though it was way too hot for a blanket. Couldn't see to go back. The only place to head was across Deep River—the old stream of trouble.

Cake saw a ferry. He called out, but there didn't seem to be anybody there to hear him. But then from the shadows appeared a hooded ferryman, the creepiest-looking something Cake had ever seen.

"Man, you near 'bout scared me to death," Cake said, shivering from head to foot. " 'Cept I'm already dead." And he chuckled in spite of himself.

The ferryman held out his skeletal hand for payment. But Cake didn't have a cent. Then he remembered something the old folks used to do—they'd always put a coin in a dead person's pocket. Most of them had forgotten why; they just did it. Cake searched his own pockets, hoping somebody had kept with tradition. Sure enough, he found a penny, and it was enough to pay the ghostly ferryman.

To quiet his nerves and bolster his courage, Cake played his harmonica as he rode across Deep River. Many a lost soul heard the music as it rose on the night wind, and they stopped crying and gnashing their teeth. "Hush, Cake Norris is playing tonight," they whispered in the darkness. "Hush. And be still."

When Cake reached the other shore, he saw a tall, inky imp with large, bat-shaped gossamer wings standing beneath the neon sign. "Come on in," it said, flashing a crooked, jagged-tooth smile. "Make yo'self comfortable while I get you properly registered."

Cake took a seat on a hard rock, and the imp pulled out a book. When Cake read the title—*The Lower Half: Stations Forty-nine to Zero*—he felt like crying, but he was too scared. "Are you Scratch?" he asked cautiously.

"Oh, noooo! No, I'm Rufus, the head crew chief in charge over everything."

"Am I one of the fallen?" Cake asked, wiping his brow.

"Not exactly," said the imp, peering down his nose. "But you're on real shaky ground." And he chuckled. It sounded wicked.

Cake couldn't help but notice that without the glasses Rufus could have been Roscoe's twin brother. Roscoe also had a better dentist.

Rufus went on to explain how things worked in his jurisdiction. "See, I'm in charge of the stations below fifty. When you're not good enough to be up there, they send you to me."

"But I aine such a bad guy," said Cake. "I did right by my mama— most of the time. And—"

"Yes, we know your story. You aine all bad, but by the time we finish with you here, you'll be just as mean and nasty as all the other folks on their way to . . ."

"Zero."

"Yes indeed, zero. The Nothing, the Great Void. Bottomless Pit. Whatever."

Rufus produced a small knife and pricked Cake's finger until it bled. "Sign your admission papers," he ordered.

As soon as Cake had used his blood to make the *s* in *Norris*, Rufus snatched up the papers and began giving him the ground rules. "Now, you needn't come down here causing confusion. We have strict orders that must be followed. And we will not tolerate anything less. I'm gon' have my eyes on you. Understood?"

"Yes, sir!"

Rufus led Cake through the doors of station twenty-five, gave him a shovel, and ordered him to join the crew that was cleaning out the horse stables of Hades. Terrible job. And stinky!

Cake's eyes searched the forever night, trying to find a familiar face—or at least a friendly one. He recognized lots of people he'd met in his life, and he nodded to them. They scoffed angrily, shrugged indifferently, or dropped their heads in shame.

Cake felt a slap on his back. "Cake! Man, I heard you was coming." It was big Lee Dumas, a semipro boxer from Detroit.

Cake let out a whoop. "Lee, if you aine a sight for sore eyes," he said, all the while pumping his friend's hand. "How long has it been?"

"Near 'bout eight years. Been here three years come October—whenever that is. I wish I'd listened to my mama and lived a better life. It's a nightmare here."

"Worse than Lee County, South Carolina?" Cake asked, managing a smile.

"Just about," Lee answered.

Stepping out of the dark, Rufus materialized. "I figured you two would be at each other's throats by now," he said.

Lee and Cake just stood there, trying to figure out what Rufus was talking about. Then Lee remembered. "He must be thinking of that fight we had over in Charleston 'bout that girl . . . what was her name?"

"Glorimae Bostic," Cake said, shaking his head. "Seems I threw the first punch. Man, I'm sorry. She wasn't worth it."

"We're okay," Lee said, rubbing his jaw, all the time recalling the punch he'd taken. "New day, a fresh deck."

Rufus was furious. "Cake, did you just apologize? Apologize! Nobody ever apologizes below station fifty. Nobody!"

"Is he always like this?" Cake whispered.

"Forevermore," said Lee.

Before Cake could say another word, he was busted up to station thirty-five.

Cake was happy to be headed upward again, until Rufus told him his assignment. "You will shovel coal on the hellbound train, twenty-four hours a day, seven days a week."

It was much hotter and with longer hours than the work at station twenty-five.

"It seems harder now that I've been busted up. Why?" Cake asked Rufus, gazing into the gloom.

"The road downhill is always easier than the one you have to climb up," Rufus explained.

Porch Lies

After dimming the lights, Rufus left. Smothering heat enveloped Cake.

"See if you can hold on to your good humor now," he heard Rufus's voice echo.

✖✖✖✖

Cake didn't recognize a single soul in this dreary place, but he felt like he knew them all. They reminded him of people he'd seen walking down the street, sitting in a restaurant, working at a filling station, or driving a bus.

He tried calling out his name. "I'm Cake Norris. Anybody know me? Do I know any of you?"

"Shut up," said one angry voice.

"Save your breath," complained another.

"It's too hot to talk," griped another.

Cake heard picks hitting against the black rock and shovels heaving up stones and throwing them onto a railcar. "Hey, down home in Alabama, this feels like sweater weather," Cake spoke into the darkness.

Somebody snickered. Then others remembered being just as hot in their old hometowns in Alabama, Mississippi, Georgia, Tennessee, and Arkansas.

"No, no, no!" a worker insisted. "Houston, Texas, is the hottest place in the world." A half-dozen folks agreed.

"If I knew then what I know now, I wouldn't have left my sweet, sweet home in Georgia," said a worker.

"What I wouldn't give to be on my grandmother's porch again, drinking iced tea and eating tea cakes," another worker added.

"We used to tell stories on my front porch," said Cake, "like this one about Sam the Sardine Man." And he began to unwind one of his famous yarns about a sardine salesman he once met in Virginia.

Before anybody knew it, two hours had passed.

Then another worker started up. "This here is a true story," he said, all soft-like. "I remember back when I was a boy in Franklin, Tennessee, I had a dog named Only. Named him that 'cause he was the only thing I had to call my own."

The story of Only was a four-hour journey through a man's childhood, but along the way, the workers laughed, cried, and cheered for a dog and a boy none of them had known but all had come to care about.

Another storyteller told 'bout the time she took a shortcut to school and fell in the creek with her clothes on. She hung them on a branch to dry, but it started raining. . . .

The sound of laughter reached every corner of holding station thirty-five. Fear sprang into the hearts of the impish guards, who'd never heard such music before. They ran to tell Rufus.

"How dare they have fun surrounded by all this misery?" Rufus growled furiously. "It's Cake Norris's fault, that—that troublemaking rascal!" And he bit a rusty nail in two, because he was just that angry.

Rufus was smart enough to realize that if this situation got out of control, it might cause him trouble with his boss, the Devil himself. And it wasn't a good time—Rufus was hoping for a promotion, or at least a bonus.

So he quietly moved Cake Norris up to holding station forty-seven. "Let's see if you got time to make people happy here," he said with a smirk.

Porch Lies

✕✕✕✕

Cake knew that station forty-seven was bound to be rough, because it was farther away from zero. He suspected Rufus was trying to harden his spirit and make him suitable for the lower levels.

While waiting for his assignment, Cake played his harmonica. It was a simple tune with minor chords that weighed heavy on the heart.

Just as Cake expected, Rufus put him on a detail digging diamonds and emeralds and other precious stones with handmade picks and shovels. And it was no longer hot, but miserably cold.

At first, Cake's spirits were mighty low. His toes were cold, his nose was cold, even his eyelids felt frozen. He thought about crying, but then thought better of it because his tears might freeze. Instead, he rubbed his hands together to warm them.

But 'fore long, he was feeling better. "If you've ever been on a Louisiana chain gang, then you know this aine so bad," he said to his fellow sufferers. "I once was told by a rail-splitter that singing makes your burden lighter. Wonder if it's true. Let's see. . . ."

And Cake began to sing.

> "Aine gonna let
> This pick and shovel
> Get me down.
> Huh!"

"I remember that song," said one man.
"I know it, too," put in another.

A few people joined in. And some more. Soon the entire mining crew was singing and digging.

> "Aine gonna let
> This pick and shovel
> Get me down.
> Huh!
> No, no.
> Aine gonna let
> This pick and shovel
> Get me down.
> Huh!
> Aine gonna let
> This pick and shovel,
> Aine gonna let
> This pick and shovel,
> Aine gonna let this pick and shovel
> Get me down.
> Huh!"

They sang so long and so loud, the guards came to see what was going on.

"They're making the strangest sound," an imp groaned to Rufus. "Aine never heard such a noise. Hurts my ears."

"The people aine the same," complained his partner. "They're not as miserable. Oh, it's depressing. Come see for yourself."

Rufus flew into a rage when he heard the singing. Immediately, he snatched Cake Norris out of the line. "I'm gon' boil you in hot oil and skin you alive, boy!"

Cake shifted from foot to foot. "Sorry, boss, but last I checked, I was dead."

"I'll banish you to a place so awful, you'll—"

"Meaning no disrespect, boss, but aine this station right here just about bad as it gets?" And Cake smiled.

The head crew chief in charge over everything picked up the phone. "Roscoe? This is Rufus. I'm sending Cake Norris back to you," he screamed in a rage. "He can't stay here!"

"No way," answered Roscoe. "Cake aine good enough to be up here. I busted him down as far as he could go."

"Well, he aine bad enough to be with us. And I've busted him up as far as he can go. Come down here apologizing, telling stories, and singing. Making people feel better. You know I can't let that go on."

"Where is he now?"

"I'm sending him up to station forty-nine—Hell's kitchen— soon as I get finished here."

What to do? What to do?

"I know," said Rufus, hatching an idea on the spot. "We can send him back to Earth. Let people deal with him there."

"We don't have the authority to do that," Roscoe argued. "We have to get permission from Death. And I aine particular 'bout bothering him, if you know what I mean."

"I do, dear brother, I do. But we have to think of something, or none of our stations will ever be the same. We have our reputations to protect."

Rufus was convincing, so they went to find Death. He lived in a distant cave on the other side of Never, on the border of station fifty.

In Never, twilight reigned twenty-four hours a day. Real nervous-like, Roscoe rang the doorbell.

"Who dares to disturb me?" said the Grim Reaper, stirring from sleep.

"Us. Roscoe . . ."

"And Rufus. Sir, we need you to send a man back to Earth."

"What? What's this nonsense?" Death was annoyed. His eyes turned cinder red in their skeletal sockets. "If a human returns to life after he's been dead and buried, other mortals will think they might do likewise."

Roscoe and Rufus took turns telling Death the problems they'd had with Cake Norris.

"He aine good enough or bad enough to be in either place," said Roscoe.

Death chuckled, but the sound was raspy from lack of use. "Cake Norris, you say? Plays a harmonica rather well?"

"That's the one. Do you know him?" Roscoe asked gingerly.

Death nodded. "Met him at a crossroads years ago. As I recall, he challenged me to a chess game, which he won. Yes, I know that rascal." And to their surprise, old Death smiled.

Just then the smell of hot chili peppers came wafting out of station forty-nine and reached all the way to Never. Death grabbed hold of Roscoe and Rufus, and they all rushed off to see what in blazes was going on.

When they got to the station, there stood none other than Cake Norris, holding the keys to Rufus's private storeroom in one hand and a ladle in the other. Seemed he had fixed a mean batch of Texas chili in a bottomless pot, and was having a fine old time, spooning it out by the gallon.

The chilis were so hot, they had set every soul on fire, but Cake had that under control, too. To cool off every blistering tongue, he was offering homemade ice cream complete with fresh peaches.

Cake had rolled up the carpet and folks from both sides of the holding stations were laughing, singing, dancing, playing cards, and telling porch lies.

Rufus ordered Cake to stop the party immediately. But even Cake couldn't bring order to the chaos he'd caused. He just shrugged and smiled.

"See what I mean?" Roscoe complained to Death.

Death stood there watching the elevators go up and down and up and down, while souls poured in and out as if on a holiday. He snickered in spite of himself.

Wasn't long before the two sides were so mixed up, Rufus and Roscoe worried they might never get the dead back to where they belonged.

"You must send that man back to Earth," whined Rufus. "They're used to his shenanigans there."

But Death was still not convinced. Besides, he hadn't enjoyed anything this much in a couple of thousand years.

"Maybe we should assign Cake to *you*, Brother Death," Rufus suggested peevishly.

"I think not." Death became grim again. "Cake Norris," he said sternly, commanding the troublemaker to step on over. "For everybody's good, I'm going to let you go back to Earth. But know this: you will not be the same. Folk will not be able to see you, and you will not be able to talk to them. Only when they hear you play your blues harmonica will they know you're around."

And so it was.

✕✕✕✕

Today Cake's spirit lives on. You can hear him at every big fish fry and chili supper, or wherever people are having fun. When old men play board games and accuse each other of cheating, when story-tellers pass on history from one generation to another, and when families come together to celebrate a new life or to say farewell to one that has ended, Cake is always in their midst.

He's with children as they play and learn to share, especially if there's singing and dancing going on.

Whenever stories about Cake Norris come up—as they're bound to do—you can feel his presence. And if you listen carefully, you will hear the faint sound of a harmonica being carried on the wind.

About the Author

Patricia C. McKissack is the author of many highly acclaimed books for children, including *The Dark-Thirty: Southern Tales of the Supernatural*; *Goin' Someplace Special*, a Coretta Scott King Award winner; and *Mirandy and Brother Wind*, recipient of a Caldecott Honor and a Coretta Scott King Award. Patricia C. McKissack lives in St. Louis.

About the Illustrator

André Carrilho is a designer, a cartoonist, a caricaturist, and an illustrator. His illustrations have appeared in the *New York Times Book Review*, *Harper's*, and *Vanity Fair*, among others. This is his first book for children. André Carrilho lives in Lisbon.